The Revival and Survival

Stump Creek Baptist Church

Brent Lay

The Revival and Survival of
Stump Creek Baptist Church
Copyright © 2021 Brent Lay
A Connection Ministries Project
All rights reserved.

Publishing assistant: The Author's Mentor, www.TheAuthorsMentor.com

ISBN: 9798518662032
This book is also available in eBook format.
Additional copies are available at cost through Amazon.

PUBLISHED IN THE UNITED STATES OF AMERICA

Acknowledgements

---◆---

I have had the great privilege of serving alongside five great Pastors including Dr. Paul Williams, Dr. Larry Gilmore, Dr. Phil Jett, Bro. Ben Mandrell, and Bro. Jordan Easley. Their guidance, support, and encouragement have certainly made a difference. Bro. Mike Sanders, Bro. Bryson McQuiston, Dr. Greg McFadden, Bro. Larry Kirk, Dr. Wendell Lang, and Bro. Ron Hale have played key roles in development of this strategy in recent years. Bro. David Taylor, Bro. Dave Jackson, and Bro. Mike Johnson, my dear friends whom I served alongside at Englewood, continue to encourage me greatly.

My wife Penny, daughters Caroline and Shelby, and son Brandon (now with families of their own) have shared in the journey of more than thirty years. Their sacrificing and giving extra support allowed me to be away many evenings doing outreach. Like all ministers, I am most grateful for the support and involvement of my family in ministry. My wife Penny is truly a gift of the Lord to me and has always been a willing and supportive partner in ministry over these many years.

Finally, I want to acknowledge all those who I have had the privilege of serving with and who have served in part-time positions dedicated to outreach. They served under different titles over the years, as we tried many approaches. These people are the true pioneers used of the Lord to develop this church missionary ministry. Most importantly, they were used of the Lord to reach hundreds upon hundreds of people for all eternity!

They include:

- College Heights Baptist Church: Vicki LouAllen, Jackie Searles, Carol Brown, Jackie Diel, and Stewart Wright.
- Englewood Baptist Church: Wanda Buford, Sandy Callis, Susan Gary, Carol Courtner, Doug Godfrey, Holly Adcock, Sarah Coughlin, Anissa Moore, Jenny Haliburton, Lorraine Harlan, Tonya Butler, Jackie Eastham, Sarah Coughlin, Holly Adcock, Charlotte Dyer, Shirley King, Brooke Veteto, Lisa Brantley, Kelley Valentine, Carol Johnson, Celia Perkins.
- Parkview Baptist Church: Jenny Thorn and Diane Hoover.
- First Baptist Humboldt: Mike Sanders and Kathy Morris
- West Jackson Baptist Church: Greg Baker and Connie Perry.
- First Baptist Jackson: Emily Shipper with Peaches Waller and James Orman as her support team.

Table of Contents

Introduction: Thriving or Dying?

Do you feel it is God's will for your church to continue to decline?

Do fewer people live in your area?

If your answers are no, this book has been written for people like you.

As result of twenty-seven years of trial and error, joys and disappointments, hundreds upon hundreds of home visits, and untold hours of investment with unchurched people, this writing captures a proven strategy which works for any size church. Yes, the strategy described in this book could truly make a big difference in the future of your church.

Based on many true stories and events, this fictional book reveals a simple but profoundly different strategy that intensifies outreach. The only names that have not been changed are Mike Sanders, Larry Gilmore, and my own. I feel the Lord used my wife Penny to suggest writing in this style.

Twenty-seven years of trial and error in determining the best tool for church outreach in today's world is a long time. I came from a rich history of Sunday School growth principles. But even in the 1980's, I realized we needed to adjust our outreach methodology. Dinner Care Groups, Evangelism Groups, Cell Church Groups, and TLC groups represent some of the more than 30 approaches we tried, as well as the full spectrum of evangelism programs such as Evangelism Explosion, Continuing Witness Trainings, NET, and FAITH.

I share all of this to assure you that what you are about to read is far more than a concept based upon telephone surveys. This is based upon years of hard knocks in the real-life laboratory interacting with the unchurched. I have never been more convinced that the strategy revealed in this book should be implemented by every church.

A special thank you to Bro. Mike Sanders for his leadership in this ministry including his efforts for distribution of this publication to church leaders like you through a not for profit entity known as Connection Ministries.

Additional copies may be purchased on Amazon. As a not for profit effort, the price for the paperback edition is priced at cost. You may also order the book as a Kindle eBook. In all sincerity, please know that this effort is not about selling books. It is all about helping your church.

God bless you and may God bless your church!

1

Goodbye, Sally Mae

Sally Mae French had been the matriarch of Stump Creek Baptist Church. Her dad had deeded property for the church 87 years prior.

Sally Mae French was regarded by all as a fine Christian lady. She had done many good things for so many and was best known for playing the piano for the church for more than 60 years since she was 12 years old. Like some other older people of the area, she did not survive the Covid-19 virus.

Sally Mae passed at age 92. A former pastor, Bro. Norman Callahan, shared in the service with the current pastor of three years, Bro. James Fields. Because of the Covid protocol, only twenty-one people were in attendance and all family units were scattered several feet apart, as seated by the funeral directors. Under different circumstances, hundreds of people would have been in attendance. The Covid-19 pandemic made a sad day even sadder. Both pastors alluded to the faithfulness of Mrs. French and the fond memories of the history of the church.

They told of her father, known as "Moon"

Mullins, who had donated the 14 acres next to the creek and helped build the original church building. The history of the church site included a huge camp meeting taking place near the creek in 1803, just two years after the landmark event of the second Great Awakening in America known as Cain Ridge Revival, which took place about 70 miles away. Reports of the time stated that as many as 2,000 people attended the two-week camp meeting, traveling as far as 100 miles.

As history has it, a large stump served as the pulpit during the camp meeting days. To keep the tradition, the Stump Creek Baptist Church always kept a stump near the creek ready for their annual homecoming service. The last stump was prepared in 1987 by cutting down a tree near the creek. It served well but was smaller than the stumps preceding it. The gentle slope of the ground upward from the creek served as a nice amphitheater for huge gatherings to both see and hear well. Both pastors expressed how those homecomings taking place on the third Sunday in May each year were very memorable events.

For years, they had outdoor services on those Sundays as weather permitted. Keeping with the tradition, the pastor or guest preacher stood on the old stump as he preached.

Bro. Norman told a story how he stepped off the stump several times one homecoming Sunday and the ladies on the front row of lawn chairs gasped and hollered each time thinking he was about to jump on them. He related with a smile that it was one of the most memorable and Spirit-filled services he had ever preached.

"Looking back, I should have jumped off that stump a little more often," he said jokingly.

Many famous preachers traveled through in days dating back prior to the Civil War, according to the oral history. About 50 yards upstream from the stump next to the creek was what locals referred to as the water hole. Even to this day, kids swim in it during the summer when the water is up.

There was an old picture on the wall above the table in the foyer the day when 32 people were baptized in the water hole after a two-week revival meeting at the church in September of 1948. The church was one of the oldest churches still active in Bacon County, Kentucky.

Pastor Fields announced the following Sunday after Mrs. French's death that he felt led to resign. He explained that the Lord had opened an opportunity for him to serve as a chaplain at a hospital in Georgia. He also mentioned that he realized the church would struggle to pay his salary.

Sally Mae had given a portion of her estate 10 years prior to make sure the church would remain open. That funding, which had been paying half of the salary for the pastor, was now depleted. The church attendance had dwindled from the twenty range to twelve or less in the past year as five members had passed and three others had moved to nursing homes near family.

Goodbye, Sally Mae French, goodbye to Pastor Fields, and maybe, goodbye to the beloved Stump Creek Baptist Church.

2

The Reckoning

The former pastor, 72-year-old Bro. Norman Callahan, agreed to supply on a Sunday-to-Sunday basis. He was good friends to the remnant of folks left having served the church for fourteen years from 1968 to 1982. During his tenure, the church grew from 140 range to 200 range in worship attendance.

Two deacons were left of the 12 regular attenders. Those two were Will Dodd and Herman Anderson, both who were older gentlemen. Herman was a retired farmer. Will was a surveyor. Both had high school educations and knew the Bible well. They asked to meet with Bro. Norman about the future of the church. Bro. Norman suggested meeting with the Baptist Association Director of Missions, Bro. Roger Stone and their State Convention consultant, Bro. Bruce Robey about what they should do.

The meeting was arranged and led to a recommendation that they should consider "dying in dignity." Bro. Roger shared that the church property would revert to Sally Mae's cousin who owned the surrounding property. Years previously, someone had shared a copy of the church deed with him that included a conversion clause which provided that the property donated to the church would revert if it was not used as a church. Bro. Robey suggested that any remaining assets could be donated to the Association or to the State Convention for the purpose of planting new churches.

At the meeting, Herman was overcome with emotion at the thought of the church closing. He broke down at the end of their meeting saying, "Fellows, I just cannot stand all this talk about our church dying. The Lord said He would build His church and the gates of hell would not prevail against it."

Will Dodd added, "It does not seem right; churches are for growing not dying. We have all kinds of people moving into this area. Why would it be better to haul off and try to raise money to build a new one when our buildings are nice and already paid for?"

Bro. Robey, the state consultant, responded with a smile. "Yes, but this is a new day. New church plants have the best chance of reaching new people. God's church will not die; just Stump Creek Baptist. This way you can die as a church with dignity and become a legacy church."

Herman and Will looked at each other with tears in their eyes, shaking their heads as if to say no.

Bro. Roger expressed that he knew this was a difficult decision and they should take their time. He assured them that they had their prayers. With that, the meeting ended with a word of prayer by Bro. Roger, the Director of Missions.

Brent Lay

3

The Dilemma

Herman and Will decided it would be best to tell the rest of the regular attendees as soon as possible about this apparent inevitable demise. Nine of the last thirteen active members were ladies. Hazel McComb, the church clerk, housekeeper, and financial secretary had served part-time for the last 20 years for the same $50-per-week salary. Liz Holland, the oldest member, had taught Sunday School for 52 years. Her class had even been named for her. Of the other seven ladies, two of those were sisters: Mildred Key and Earline Evans. Rose King, a fifty-year member, had always been the director of the children's ministry, including heading up annual Vacation Bible Schools. Gordon, Sr., and Sadie Hadley were some of the oldest members. Gordon, Sr., was a cancer patient who had been in and out of the hospital several times in recent months. Gordon Hadley, Jr. and his wife Pam, were the youngest active members (in their 50's). Clarice was Herman's wife. Will's wife, Jan, had served the church well as a ladies' teacher over the years, but could not attend regularly because of her

Parkinson's disease.

The Wednesday night meeting designated for the purpose of discussing the future of Stump Creek was attended by all twelve regular attendees. Bro. Herman called the meeting to order and described the outcome of the meeting with Bro. Roger Stone and Bro. Bruce Robey. He explained that he did not have a peace about it as he frowned and looked down.

Liz Holland stood with the help of her walker parked next to the pew and said, "We need to start praying for a way through."

Will replied, "We have been praying, and certainly all of us need to pray about this more. We need a miracle. It just seems too late. Look at us. All of us except for Gordon Hadley, Jr., and his wife Pam are over 70 years old."

Gordon, Sr., and Sadie Hadley were some of the oldest members in terms of age. Gordon, Sr., did not profess Jesus as his Savior until he was 75 years old (fifteen years prior). Their son, Gordon Hadley, Jr., who also was gloriously saved about two weeks after his dad at age 40, served as the volunteer music leader.

As everyone glanced around at each other, Will added, "We might as well face it, churches, like people, live and die."

Liz insisted on more prayer.

Rose said, "Pastor Norman is a good soul and I

think if we ask, he will continue to supply preach for us even if we cannot pay him much. And I will cook Sunday dinner every other Sunday for him, to boot, if he will help us for a few more weeks."

All agreed to ask Bro. Norman to continue to supply preach and dedicated their Wednesday meeting times for prayer and further deliberation about the future of the church.

Brent Lay

4

Rose's Reflections

Over the next few Wednesday nights, only seven showed up at one time. Bro. Norman agreed to come every Sunday morning and be present as they needed him every other Wednesday night. They had discontinued the Sunday night services about four years previously since most of the membership could not see well enough to drive at night.

As the third Wednesday night came around, Rose King wanted to reminisce the past and all the great victories. She had made notes in her prayer journal referring to it as she spoke. She went into detail about the wonderful revivals, as well as fond memories of the fish fries, picnics on the grounds, the homecomings, and even the watermelon cuttings after church on Sunday nights.

Mildred Key said, "Don't forget all those great homemade hot rolls served at our Wednesday night fellowship meals."

Clarice spoke up and added, "I haven't forgotten those rolls. Herman gained 20 pounds during those days. I think about those homemade rolls often when I see Herman's bare belly."

All started laughing, and one by one, shared stories about the past with tears flowing down their checks from time to time.

Rose chimed back in. "Those sure were good times in the Lord. Folks were saved. We had a big Vacation Bible School each summer. Many times over a hundred were in attendance."

Will said fondly, "Rose, you always did have a big rear-view mirror."

"Well, Will," she replied, "When you have watched more than 200 of our children grow up in this church, there is a lot to remember! Three of our children became missionaries overseas, two became preachers, and one continues to serve full-time as a minister of music at a church in North Carolina."

Hazel added, "Homecomings on the third Sundays in May have always been very special times for me. So many people to this day, even in other states, want to be reminded so they can make plans to attend."

Over the next few Wednesday nights, it seemed soothing to dwell on the past. Some brought pictures and Hazel suggested putting pictures together and have copies made at a local printer so they could have a church memorial book, like folks do at funerals. Yes, it seemed as if they were funeral planning for the church.

Lots of young folks were building houses around the old church, but of those who went to church, most attended the Fresh Water Church which was eight miles away, known for loud music, big screens, and even smoke machines.

Mildred Key said, "It is such a shame to close our doors. What did we do wrong?"

Will said, "Bro. Roger, our DOM, explained why the newer churches can draw the people. I think he will be willing to come on a Wednesday night and share. After all, it may be our last time together with him and it will give us a chance to say goodbye."

5

Preparing for an Autopsy

Bro. Roger Stone, whom they all loved, had served 32 years as the DOM (Director of Missions) of their Association of Churches, which covered an area of two counties. He agreed to come the very next Wednesday night.

After some delicious hot apple pie and coffee, they sat around the tables in the corner of the fellowship hall. Their fellowship hall was one of the newer wings of the church built about thirty years previously and had the capacity to seat 150. On special occasions, they had to eat in shifts, but now they only had three eight-foot round tables set up.

Bro. Roger began by saying, "So much has changed in our years together. The methods we used to reach people do not seem to work anymore. Sunday school, for the most part, has gone by the wayside. Dr. Ryder at Lifeway says most of the churches like yours are going to close in the next few years. It's just a sign of the times."

Gordon, Sr., spoke up asking, "Did you say the Lifeway Doctor? Is that the new bus for blood donations?"

"No, no," said Bro. Roger. "Dr. Ryder is not a medical doctor. He is an expert on church growth and until recently, he worked at Lifeway, which used to be the old Sunday School Board."

Gordon, Sr., responded, "You mean to tell me they have already closed down the Sunday School Board?"

"No, no," said Bro. Roger. "It's still going, they just renamed it a few years ago. But Lifeway has been downsizing. They sold the big buildings in Nashville to build a new smaller one and now they are selling Ridgecrest, too."

"Oh, my!" said Hazel. "We used to go every year to Ridgecrest with a van full. That was one of the best things our convention ever had. What is this world coming to?"

Bro. Roger responded, "I agree; it is kind of sad."

Bro. Herman said, "I got the impression from Bro. Bruce Robey that overall, things are going great with all the new church starts."

Bro. Roger said, "We are proud of all the new starts. Churches in our association are helping 12 or so now. Most are out of state. But overall, our numbers for baptisms and membership in our Southern Baptist Convention continue to decline. Our convention recently hit a 50-year low in baptisms. Most predict that ten thousand churches of the more than forty-five thousand total will close in the next ten to fifteen years."

"Wow," said Bro. Herman. "At least our Association is growing. I know we have three big churches that have over 400 attending."

"Yes, we can celebrate for those three churches," said Bro. Roger. "And that is where most of our young people are going. At least 7 of our 31 churches will probably close in the next five years. Unfortunately, they are in the same boat as you. Their churches are literally dying as many of their people are getting in bad health as they grow older."

Bro. Roger continued to share how he had been to a conference recently. He reflected with them that the same pattern of smaller churches closing was true across the South. He explained, "For years, the smaller churches have had their younger members going to the larger churches. They usually have better children's programs and better music because they have the financial support. The better they do, the more church folks come. Unfortunately, the numbers tell us that it is generally folks from the smaller churches who are joining the larger churches. We know this because our overall numbers for our Association are less than they were 30 years ago. But, as you well know, our county has doubled in population over the last 30 years."

Rose said, "That is really sad. What you are saying is that we mostly have traded sheep over these years."

Bro. Roger smiled and said, "Yes, that is one way of describing our situation. But God is in charge and He is able. I am not saying you should give up. I have to admit though, I do not know what to tell you. The outlook for many churches like yours is not good."

Gordon Hadley, Jr., leaned in and said, "Bro. Roger, the way I see it, we may have done nothing wrong, but it seems we missed the boat somehow. We have had some really good preachers since Pam and I have been here, and the part-time young fellow leading our music with a guitar before I took over was really good. He has several successful CD's. If it is not our preaching, and not our music, do you think it's just our bad breath?"

Everybody laughed.

Bro. Roger said, "If I knew the answer to that question, I would be a very rich man."

Bro. Will joined in the conversation saying, "It probably has to do with our outreach. Back in the old days, we spent an enormous amount of time adding to our Sunday School rolls, visiting homes, and going door to door, inviting folks to our spring and fall revivals. In those days, we had to go out and make friends before they tried out our church. You would think there would be a way we could greet and meet people like we did in the past."

No one else spoke up.

In closing the discussion, Bro. Roger shared,

"Dying with dignity and transferring any assets has become the recommended path for many churches like Stump Creek."

All took turns praying out loud during a closing prayer time. A sob could be heard from time to time. The most recurring prayer line was, "Lord, show us Your way. We don't want to close up, Lord, but we will if You tell us to…"

Brent Lay

6

Finding the Band-Aid™ Box

Old Bro. Norman came faithfully to preach the 10:30 Sunday morning service and as a widower, he enjoyed going to Rose King's home for Sunday lunch. Rose's husband, Noel (also one of the deacons) had passed 7 years before. She asked that one of the deacons always join him when he visited. Most times, that would be Herman and wife Clarice, because Will's wife Jan could rarely attend anymore with her oncoming Parkinson's disease.

One Sunday after a wonderful sermon from Luke 15 about the lost sheep, the lost coin, and the lost son, Bro. Norman, Herman, and Clarice joined Rose for lunch. After the usual cuisine of fried chicken and a melody of vegetables, Rose served big slices of her famous coconut cake. It included a creamed cheese concoction between the layers and was always a big-time favorite at church homecoming meals. People use to go to get slices of her cake before they even started eating their meal because if they didn't, it could be gone before they were ready for dessert.

Sipping strong coffee and lip smacking while

partaking of the coconut cake, Clarice turned to Bro. Norman and said, "Herman and I love you so much and I do not want to burden you, but I need for you to hear me out about a dream I had night before last. Today, you preached about the lost coin and I know with all my heart that God was speaking to me night before last."

With a smile, Bro. Norman said, "Well, sister Clarice, you know I will be glad to hear you and answer any questions that I think I am able."

"Well," Clarice said, "it all started when I lost my Band-aid box on Thursday."

"Jumpin' Jehoshaphat!" Bro. Herman laughed out loud. "Oh, Lord, Clarice, surely all this earnestness of matter is about more than an old Band-aid box. You had me worried there for a minute."

Rose clapped her hands and said, "Oh, this is going to be good, I can tell. Go on, Clarice. Tell us, dear."

"What Herman doesn't know is that I have been bad about forgetting things the last year or so. I started putting my valuable jewelry and cash money, about a thousand dollars, in an old metal Band-aid box."

Herman said, "Oh, no. Don't tell me you've lost it or thrown it away."

"Now, Herman," said Clarice, "this is my story; let me tell it. It is important, I say. I had a hard time sleeping Thursday night and after looking all day Friday for the Band-aid box, I went to bed praying about it. I would have told Herman, but I thought he would have us tearing up the house looking for it all night! I must have prayed for three hours before I fell asleep. I awoke Saturday morning remembering a dream. I was asking the Lord to show me where my Band-aid box was. I was giving Him all the reasons I needed to find it. I told Him I would never take off my ring again or keep cash around the house if only I could find it."

"Tell us what the Lord said," prompted Rose.

"Well, I felt the Spirit of the Lord say, 'Clarice, don't you see?' If only you were as concerned about My church as you are about your Band-aid box. Remember the widow searching for the lost coin? She searches diligently and asks friends to join her...' Then I recalled while still in my dream that there is more joy in Heaven over one lost sheep who gets saved than the ninety-nine in the fold. When you preached that passage this morning, it struck my heart that God was truly speaking to me in my dream."

Herman asked, "Did the Lord tell you where that Band-aid box was?"

"Yes, indeed. I found it in the pantry first thing Saturday morning. I remembered just as I reached to fix the coffee."

"Well, that is good" replied Herman.

"Changing the subject, this sure is some good cake, Rose."

Clarice said, "Herman, you are missing the point. God has given me and us a word. Just like we have been praying for since we started those Wednesday night prayer times. Don't you think it's true, Bro. Norman? Or do you think, I am just going crazy in old age?"

"Clarice, my dear saint, you are preaching a better sermon than I did this morning. God's good Word tells us that God speaks in various and sundry ways. Many times, we know His Word speaks of hearing the Lord in dreams. Yes, indeed, I think you have received a word from the Lord. He wants you to do something. I think one of the first things to do is to share this with your Wednesday night prayer warriors. What God says to one He will say to others. The Lord only leads in one direction at a time."

After pleasantries, Herman, Clarice, and Bro. Norman graciously left.

Clarice called that very afternoon the others who usually came on Wednesday evenings and told them she would like to have time to share about her dream.

The next Wednesday, she went over every detail. The ladies were delighted, and the men glanced at each other as if there was too much drama going on. Nevertheless, during the prayer time, each thanked the Lord for guidance and prayed a theme: "Lord, show us thy own way. Not our way, Lord, only thy way."

Will added as a benediction, "Lord, please do not tarry much longer. You know, Lord, our funds are getting short."

That was the truth of the matter. Hazel had asked Bro. Norman to wait to cash his $100 Wednesday check until after she could make the Sunday offering deposit on Monday. The bank balance was running less than $100.

Brent Lay

7

Wrong Turn in Romans?

Once each month on the first Sunday afternoon, the deacons always held a meeting. Even though only two of them were left, it seemed only right to meet anyway with Bro. Norman. Bro. Norman told them he would be glad to circle back from Rose King's lunch and meet them about 2 p.m. at the church. They reviewed a copy of the bank statement showing an $82 balance for the end of the previous month.

Will said, "We used to keep a $20,000 balance with a $200,000 budget."

Herman said, "Bro. Norman, unless you can tell us different, it looks like we only have a few more weeks. Just one or two of us going to the nursing home or dying is surely going to mean the end of our church."

"Confidentially," said Herman, "Will and I have been chipping in extra money to keep our buildings up. It has only been God's grace that we have had the finances to get by."

Will, shaking his head, said, "You know, Bro. Norman, when you were here back 30 years ago, we saw lots of growth, lots of baptisms and did not have any financial issues. I think we have lost our way somewhere along the line."

Bro. Norman, knowing that Will could get stirred up sometimes, said, "Don't feel too bad. We have had several churches in our area and really all through the South running the same course. Things change, church is not like it used to be. The younger folks do not feel they need to go to church. Over the last 30 years, the emphasis has been more on the worship service and our Baptist Convention has more pastors believing reformed theology."

"Reformed?" said Herman. "Is that the same thing as Calvinism?"

"For the most part, yes," replied Bro. Norman.

Herman said, "Well, doesn't that just take the cake. Our churches are declining at the same time Calvinism is growing. Is that not the truth?"

"I see why you say that" replied Bro. Norman. "But that observation may not be necessarily connected. I have known some very evangelistic Baptist preachers who are Calvinists. That whole issue has been going on for years."

"Yep," said Will. "I have read all about John Gill and Andrew Fuller. Many folks in his time, back in the 1700's, referred to John Gill as the High or Hyper Calvinist, right?"

"That is correct," said Bro. Norman. "He believed that there are no universal offers of grace and salvation to all men."

"So, hyper means over the top?"

Bro. Norman laughed. "I suppose that is one way you could describe it."

Herman chipped in. "Well, I think the young pastor that followed you did not lead us well. He was smart and well-educated, but he was really into that Calvinism stuff. He made a joke a few times saying he really liked 1st, 2nd, and 3rd John best, and then he would say he meant the beliefs of John Calvin, John McArthur, and John Piper. He often told us that he preferred to disciple, not evangelize. He always said that was his strength. During the three years he was here, our attendance declined even more."

"Ah," said Will. "I tell you most of those folks take a wrong turn in the book of Romans."

"Wrong turn?" replied Bro Norman.

"Why, yes. Back in the early 1990's when we still had those week-long revivals, an old preacher from Georgia explained it. We had brown bag lunches in those days."

Herman said, "They always had some of the best homemade cookies in those brown bags with the sandwiches."

"That preacher told us he would answer any question. We spent three or four lunch sessions with him teaching us about the wrong turn he felt some make in Romans." Will continued.

Bro. Norman said, "Will, that's new for me. What in the world are you talking about?"

Will, who was a surveyor by trade, said, "You have to start at the right place to end at the right place. He said, 'I tell the fellows who work for me that all the time. If you get it wrong on the front end, you are not going to arrive at the right spot. Apostle Paul wrote to the Jews first in Romans, just as he said three times, to the Jews first, then to the Gentiles. Just look at verse 13 in the first chapter. Paul said, 'you, as well as the rest of the Gentiles.' He was saying to you the Jews first and then to the Gentiles I have yet to evangelize. Paul wrote to the Jews first in the first eight chapters and then to the Gentile believers in the last eight chapters."

Bro. Norman asked, "Why do you think Paul would want to do that?"

Will said, "Paul knew all about the major problem, the division of the Jewish believers and the Gentile believers at the church in Rome. He knew firsthand of this serious rift because he was best of friends with Aquila and Priscila. They had been expelled just we are told in Acts 18 and then returned to Rome."

"Yes," said Herman, "Will has told me about this several times and I think he has it right. If Chapters 1-8 are speaking to the Jews and not the Gentiles, then that verse saying those whom he foreknew, he predestined is just confirming what

34

the Old Testament says about God's plan for the Jews since the days of Abraham. Anyone reading chapter 9 can clearly see Paul begins to speak to the Gentiles and explains why God chose some of the Jews and temporarily hardened the others. It was God's choice to choose a portion or remnant of the Jews for His special purpose. God is the Potter."

Listening intently, Bro. Norman shook his head and said, "That is interesting. It sounds reasonable, but how can you explain Ephesians 1:5 about knowing us before the foundation of the world?"

"Well, Bro. Norman," said Herman, "that too is fairly simple. Paul is talking about himself and his companion as being of the Jews. God's Word in Deuteronomy tells us in chapter 7, verse 14, that of all the people in the world, He knew or had a special relationship with the Jewish people only. In those first verses of Ephesians, Paul clearly uses the pronoun 'we' and 'us', saying as Jewish believers, God had a purpose for them before the foundation of the world. But, in the 13th verse of that chapter one of Ephesians, Paul said 'you'. Paul is saying, 'but when you heard the Gospel.' That change of pronouns to from 'we' to 'you' is very important. The 'you' obviously referred to the Gentile believers."

"I am amazed at this," said Bro. Norman. "I am not saying you are wrong, but I can tell you I have studied this issue for a long time and I have a lot of commentaries. I do not think any of those writers agree with your take. It comes to my mind what Jesus said in John 6:37 that 'all the Father gives me will come to me' could prove your thinking wrong."

Will replied, "Bro. Norman, as you well know, the context of that entire exchange, like most of the gospel of John, involves Jesus debating the Jewish leaders. When the ministry of Jesus started, it was a transitional time between the old and new covenants. We have to keep in mind that Old Testament saints were in the presence of Jesus. I think they represented the ones God had given to Jesus. Jesus knew them and they knew Him. And He said he would not lose any except ole Judas."

Bro. Norman smiled. "Well, fellows, you know I love you, but in 50 years of ministry, I do not remember hearing this explanation. I have to say, you both make good points."

"After all these years, we Baptists are still divided on this issue. It is obvious that one side is wrong in its interpretation" said Will. "A big part of our demise is that we quit reaching people for Jesus like we did when you were here. It is a different day, but people are still dying without Jesus. I think we lost our way when we started thinking people's salvation is a done deal."

"Fellows," asserted Bro. Norman, "one thing I agree on is that our methodology follows our theology. Sharing the Gospel with others can get put on the backburner quickly. If you or any church does not have the enthusiasm and heart for it, it usually does not happen."

"Amen," replied Herman.

"It's already four o'clock," said Bro. Norman, "you fellows won't do. In some ways, I'm glad we don't have nine deacons like the old days. You all would keep me all night."

They laughed and then had closing prayer. During the prayer, Bro. Norman asked the Lord to give them wisdom about everything they had discussed.

Brent Lay

8

More Joy in Heaven

Bro. Norman had been preaching for over 50 years and according to the local funeral home had preached more than 700 funeral sermons, by far the most of any preacher in the area. Most every Monday at 10 am, he met with fifteen or so other pastors at the Baptist Association office. This particular Monday, it was his turn to give a devotional. The scripture he used was from John 15:5, "he who abides in Me and I in him, he will bear much fruit."

He told the fellow pastors that morning that he had a heavy heart and needed their prayers. He humbly admitted, "I feel like I am preaching a funeral at Stump Creek these days. My wife and I saw so much good fruit during my 14 years as their pastor. We added a children's building and a fellowship hall when I was there. I could never imagine that the church would be closing just thirty years after I left. It is hard to understand. About ten times the people live within five miles of the church. You would think the church would be at least twice the size and running four hundred.

Instead, we only had eleven in attendance last Sunday."

Looking out the window, after pausing, he softly added, "Please pray for the church and pray for me. I am struggling to decide what I am going to preach this coming Sunday. It may well be the last Sunday for me to preach there."

As the week went on, Bro. Norman found himself thinking about Clarice's dream and sensed he should preach about the lost prodigal son. As he prayed, he found himself thinking more and more about the words, *more joy in Heaven than the ninety and nine*. The clearness of his message came upon him.

Yes, more joy in Heaven...

He thought that would indeed serve well as possibly the last sermon preached at Stump Creek Baptist Church. As a very accomplished funeral preacher, he always loved to conclude those sermons describing the wonderful joys of Heaven.

9

Revive Us Again

On March 7th, the aromas of spring and the excitement of warmer weather had everyone in a good mood. As Gordon, Jr., stood to lead a couple of songs out of the hymnal as customary, he said, "Since we may not be able to do this much longer, I thought I would choose one of our all-time favorite hymns which has meant so much to me over these years. *Revive Us Again*. The second song is, *He Lives*, which ends on that immortal question, 'you ask me how I know he lives; he lives within my heart.'"

When big, burly deacon Will Dodd came to do the offertory prayer, he seemed to struggle to walk. He did something that he had rarely done before, he knelt next to the pulpit on one knee. During his prayer, he kept saying, "We love You, Lord, we thank You, Lord." And then with deep emotion in his voice he said, "We don't want to die, Lord. This church belongs to You, always has. Have thy own will, Lord. You know, Lord, we don't won't to close these doors. Amen."

As Will rose with tears streaming down his

face, it was apparent that all, even Bro. Norman, had tears in their eyes.

As Bro. Norman stood to begin by reading Scripture, he said, "Saying goodbye to your church is never easy." He read the last 12 verses of chapter 15 of Luke. *"More Joy in Heaven* is the title of our message today."

As he passionately proceeded to describe the joy of the Father, he said, "It will not be long before all of us are in Heaven. What a day of rejoicing that will be! So many things we can do in Heaven; we will worship, we shall sing, and yes, we will dance in joy, and I personally think we will enjoy eating! But there is one thing we will never do in Heaven and that is tell a lost soul about Jesus."

He continued, "*More Joy is in Heaven over the one.* Think about it. In God's eyes, He is telling us that it is not about our pretty church, our preaching, our music, or even our offerings that bring Him the most joy. It is about more joy for the Father for the one. It is not about us. We are like the elder son; we already have it all in the Lord. But, oh, the *one.* Just one who is lost and now found; that brings on more joy in Heaven."

"Dear church family," he continued, "I say this to you as a church today, we can give up our gathering at Stump Creek Baptist knowing that God has a plan and a purpose. I want to share with you that last Sunday afternoon, I received a great message.   Deacon Will and deacon Herman preached a message to me like few in my life. I say this because all week, I could not get their message out of my mind nor off my heart."

Bro. Norman related, "I want to confess to you that I, like a lot of good Christian folks, sometimes become what I call *que sera, sera* Christians. We adopt the mindset *whatever will be, will be.* That includes the thinking that we do not have to feel burdened to reach out to others because their salvation is already determined."

He concluded, "Don't you see the Father is saying in this passage that we are to be devoted, dedicated and directed to go after the lost sheep. We are to search for the lost coin, earnestly pray and seek for decisions of those like the lost son?"

"I planned all week to come here today and tell you next Sunday would be my last Sunday here. I had planned to preach about letting go. But last night and even early this morning, I felt the Lord told me to preach a sermon about a new beginning. I do not know how the Lord is leading you today but when the invitation music starts, I am going to be the first to kneel here at the altar. I feel the Lord is not finished with this church. He is not through with Stump Creek. I do not know how He is going to do it, but I pledge to you I will do my part."

"Hazel, as we all stand after my prayer, please play on the piano that little song, *Yes Lord, yes, to*

Your will and to Your way."

Within a minute, all came forward to sit on one of the front pews with heads bowed. *Yes, Lord, yes, to Your will and to Your way* was taken to heart.

Things seemed normal when everyone was leaving that day, but eyes and hearts had been lifted, and each knew something significant had happened. They had hope and a new song in their hearts.

The ladies saying goodbye on the front sidewalk seemed to cheer one another as they waved goodbye, saying, "I cannot wait until Wednesday night. I can't wait to see what God is going to do!"

10

"New Wine Skins"

Bro. Norman came that next Wednesday and said he did not know the direction the Lord was leading, but he felt whatever the Lord was going to do, it would be something new. He gave a short devotion about new wineskins. He said, "We all must be diligent to get a word from the Lord. I will begin calling some of my longtime friends about any new approaches that God seems to be using." Then he reminded the group that, "after all, Sunday School was not a tool for growth of Southern Baptists until the early 1900's and God used that tool in a mighty way."

Bro. Norman went to the preachers' meeting that Monday and met separately with Bro. Roger Stone. He told him about his conviction that they needed to do something new and for him to let him know if he heard any new approaches that seemed to be working.

Bro. Roger called Bro. Norman on Thursday morning. He said, "I happened to look through my file this morning and I found a little handout entitled *The Church Missionary Movement*. The more I looked at it and then glanced at the referred website[1],

I think it might be that new approach you have been looking for."

Bro. Norman asked, "Where did that handout come from?"

"It must have come from one of our state pastors retreats a couple of years back. It looks like the three fellows listed on the website are from Tennessee. One of the fellows who wrote a forward was the State Evangelism Director at one time. His name is Larry Gilmore. He and the author, Brent Lay, appear to be retired. A fellow minister named Mike Sanders has also been involved. It says the strategy is based upon 27 years of experience. There is lots of information on the website."

"Thanks for sharing, you never know," quipped Bro. Norman. "Maybe the Lord is opening a door."

Bro. Roger said, "I sure hope so, Bro. Norman. I feel the Lord is working through you. I have not seen you so excited about starting something in years. You have all the other pastors talking. They joke that you must have got on Geritol or be smoking something. For you even to suggest Stump Creek stay open and try something new has them shaking their heads. You know, I am praying for you and the church."

Bro. Norman begin viewing the website within minutes. He was impressed that the approach was based upon 27 years of development by Brent Lay,

[1] www.churchmissionarymovement.com

a former Director of Missions and Minister of Education from Jackson, Tennessee. He was pleased to see that the messengers of the Tennessee Baptist Convention unanimously adopted a resolution encouraging churches in Tennessee and nationally to adopt this ministry approach at their state convention in the fall of 2015. He viewed a YouTube video of this action per a link provided on the website.

He later spent hours reading the articles, the training manual, and ministry description which were also on the website. The website included contact information which asked that a short church profile be forwarded to Brent Lay or an assigned consultant.

The next day, he received a call from Bro. Mike Sanders, one of the consultants. Bro. Norman and Bro. Mike agreed that the next step would be having a conference call on the phone with the Wednesday night group at the church. By the next day, Bro. Norman was able to confirm that meeting. He downloaded several pages about the ministry from the website and handed out the packets of information the next Sunday morning. asking each to review and study it before their scheduled meeting on Wednesday.

Bro. Mike spent most the time in this introductory meeting highlighting points in the written material. He said usually it worked best for everyone to study the material and hold most of the questions for a future meeting. Mike explained that a first step would be to form a missions team (or committee) and for that group to focus upon allocating or securing funds that would be used to compensate the part-time positions that paid for about eight to ten hours per week. He shared that the cost would be around $8,000 per position, per year, and that he usually recommended three positions. He added that two positions could be a starting point. After answering four or five questions at the end of his presentation, the meeting was concluded.

11

Hitting a Wall...Not Enough Money

Bro. Herman began the next Wednesday night meeting telling the group he was convinced the church missionary or connection ministry might work for Stump Creek, but then added, "I don't think it is going to happen because we just don't have that kind of extra money."

"Exactly, how much money does it take," asked Rose.

"If we do three connection coordinators, or church missionaries as Bro. Mike suggested to Bro. Norman, we will need $24,000 the first year."

Will said, "That answers that. Our total giving now comes out to be only about $40,000 a year."

Hazel interjected, "Did not Mike say that we might start with only two missionaries?"

"He did say that," added Bro. Norman and then explained. "It boils down to paying a stipend of $150 per week for each part-time missionary serving 8 hours per week. Even with two part-time positions, we would have to raise $16,000 beyond our regular giving."

"Goodness, that is going to be a big stretch for us, because most of us are living on social security income," replied Herman.

Rose spoke up. "Bro. Norman, do we really believe this could work?"

Bro. Norman smiled and said slowly, "It is new to me, but based on everything I have heard, I think it is for real. Mike even gave me three ladies to call who did this ministry for years. Their stories are convincing. It reminds me of the old days when we had a welcome-wagon lady for anyone new who moved into our town. Like Mike told us, it is about connecting the folks outside the church with the folks inside the church."

Will joined in saying, "What I like about this initiative is interacting with lost people first and not waiting until someone comes to church. Waiting for folks to come to our church has not worked in years."

Sadie questioned, "Is not this what we as church members should be doing anyway? Do we need to be paying people to do what we are supposed to be doing?"

They all looked at Bro. Norman. He smiled and said, "You paid me for many years to do all types of outreach ministry and never had a problem with it. Most churches pay folks to clean the church, to work in the nursery, and play the piano. The fact of the matter is, connecting with unchurched people is hard work. It involves lots of hours dealing with strangers. Truth is, most of us, even preachers, had rather spend our free time with friends. If there is a way for us to start this ministry, each of us will have to be involved to some degree, but I also think that the coordination of an effective outreach will require a special effort. We have an opportunity with this ministry to put our money where our heart is, so to speak."

He continued, "Missionary work by definition is crossing barriers with the Gospel, and the Lord knows we have a lot of new people that have moved in around here that are a lot different from us. That means there are lots of barriers."

Hazel said, "Besides all that, Bro. Norman, we are old!"

Everyone laughed.

"It seems like we should try it, but I guess it is no use beating a dead horse," said Herman. "If we cannot afford it, we just cannot afford it."

"Hold on, Herman," piped up Gordon, Jr. "I suggest we keep an open mind and continue to pray about it. The bad news is maybe we cannot afford it. But the good news is this may be the one thing standing between us closing or staying open and reaching people for years to come. If God is in this, $16,000 per year is doable."

Herman responded, "I am willing to keep

praying about it. Let's come together again next Wednesday and maybe we can decide. But remember, right now we just do not have the money. This is a mountain to climb. We have been blessed to have maintained our buildings and stayed within our budget as it is."

"Let each of us continue to pray about how God would have us respond," said Rose.

Everyone nodded in the affirmative and the meeting was closed with a prayer led by Bro. Norman.

12

Smiles in Heaven

Bro. Herman started the meeting the next Wednesday by saying, "To be realistic, we cannot try this approach unless we can fund it for at least eighteen months. I remember Bro. Mike telling us that it took about six months before any new members joined. Plus, remember he said that new Christians usually do not start tithing until after the first year. I say all of this to say we need about $32,000 to pay for the stipends to the church missionaries for the next two years."

Will said shaking his head, "That is a little more than $300 per week."

Hazel said, "The Lord and I have had some long talks this week, and I do not have much, but all I have is His. I told the Lord last week when I left that I would give the $50 the church has been paying me. I use that money for groceries when my grandkids come and to buy Christmas presents, but I am sure my family will understand. All three of my children were baptized in this church and two of them were married here."

Hazel continued, "But you know the Lord kept

prodding until I finally landed on what He is telling me to do. You all know that I have had seven teeth pulled in the last twelve months. I have two more right here in front that need to be pulled soon. I have saved around $5,000 over the last four years for dental implants that I had planned to be put in next month. But I have decided I want to give that money toward this cause. The way I figure, Bro. Herman, that will mean I am pledging to give an additional $10,000 over the next two years, and I can write a check for $5,000 cash up front."

Mildred, who was sitting next to Hazel put her hand on Hazel's hand and said, "Oh, dear Hazel, you don't need to do all that. I know you have been looking forward to that new smile for a long, long time."

"I insist," said Hazel. "I have a perfect peace about it. I told the Lord; my smiles can happen in Heaven. My smiles and His joy in Heaven are far more important than my new teeth down here on this earth. The more I thought about it, I will be on the other side before too long, so I really would not get my money's worth down here anyway. Besides, I have five or six pretty masks I wear now, and if I have to have another front tooth pulled, I will just keep wearing my masks."

They all started laughing even though several had tears in their eyes. Hazel had always been willing to do for everyone else. She had always been one of the first to give of herself for her church even when her husband Paul was living. He had died at an early age when their kids were teenagers and Hazel had worked hard doing all sorts of jobs over the years to keep the bills paid.

Rose started weeping. "The Lord's been dealing with me, too! I have been struggling over the last few days because the Lord seemed to be nudging me to give above and beyond my regular giving. I was praying all week, and the Lord seem to say, 'pray and listen, pray and listen.' I was watching the evening news and a commercial came on I had seen many times before talking about a reverse mortgage on a home. My two boys have done well as you know. Don is a doctor and Dan is a banker. I called Dan last Sunday and told him I felt the Lord wanted me to do that reverse mortgage on my home so I could give a $20,000 gift to the church. He said he had a way of doing a mortgage that would work the same way. He called me this afternoon and said all the paperwork has been prepared and I could write the check this coming Sunday. So there, Hazel. I am doing this, and I am not even giving up a new smile. And I will be right beside you when we both are smiling in Heaven!"

"You ladies are plum crazy!" Herman exclaimed with a big smile. "Crazy, I say," he repeated as he rubbed his mostly bald head with both hands. "But you are crazy for the Lord."

Bro. Norman started laughing, saying, "I came to tell you I was going to give back half my honorarium for at least the next year, helping out $2,500 also, but you ladies stole all my thunder. I tell you what, I will pledge two years if you all allow me to preach that long and the good Lord gives me the days. So, Will, that's $35,000 ahead by my figures."

"Yes, it is," said Will with his hand in the air as giving praise unto the Lord.

Gordon, Jr., broke out singing, *"To God be the Glory for great things He has done."*

Others joined as they sung the all-familiar first and last verses. Everyone left rejoicing that night and some were anxious to get home and make some phone calls to tell others that $35,000 was raised in one week.

Bro. Norman told the others to start praying that the Lord provide two part-time church missionaries. "I will line up Bro. Mike Sanders to meet with us again by phone or video conference next Wednesday night. I can hardly wait to tell him what has happened!"

13

"You Have Not For You Ask Not"

Bro. Norman conferred with Herman about doing a video conference or Face Time™ call the next Wednesday night. Bro. Norman had a grandson come with him on the next Wednesday night and in short order, with nine members in attendance, the grandson had his smart phone connecting with Mike on Face Time™. He propped the phone on a table where all could see Mike, and Mike could see them.

Bro. Mike began by saying that the endeavor "begins and ends with prayer." Then he stopped and prayed for God's guidance and blessings upon their time.

Bro. Norman told Mike that he had gone by the Association Office and now all nine of them had the pages of the "Launch" section in hand.

Mike explained that he was going to spend about 30 minutes with them on the call so they would have an hour or so to discuss and work through the questions and answers in the packet.

Mike summarized the prayer section and emphasized the importance of seeking God's will and God's way at every turn. The second section was about forming the missionary team for the church. Herman volunteered an idea that since it was only nine of them who could attend regularly that they become the missionary team. All agreed.

The third section had to do with the cost and the process of securing financial support. Mike shared that he was pleased to hear that funding was already in place.

He said, "This is going to put you about two months ahead, as we usually go through a process of six to twelve weeks to secure commitment for funds to pay the part-time church missionaries or connection coordinators."

He said that the title for the people serving in these part-time positions is an option of the church.

The next section, as Mike proceeded, dealt with the process of seeking out and commissioning two people to serve in the capacity as church missionaries.

"Primarily," he emphasized, "these two people need to feel called of the Lord for this task and the team needs to sense the Lord's confirmation."

He explained that these two people do not necessarily have to be members of the church, but it would be better if they already knew about your church or were good friends with someone in the church. He referred the group to the pages which included a spiritual gift survey and personality profile.

Lastly, he went over the ministry description of the part-time position and emphasized that every church missionary carried out this ministry a little different, depending on their giftedness and opportunities within the community. The end goal for each church missionary is to connect and reach at least five family units for your church each year," said Mike. "Now for the questions."

Herman asked, "Mike, did you say a minimum of five families to be reached per year is the goal for each of our two missionaries?"

"That is correct," replied Mike, "but please keep in mind that usually we have a six-month ramp-up time. Based upon experience, I feel once your missionaries are online, you all will reach five or six families the first year and ten families the next year."

"That sounds a little strong," said Will. "We only have about fifteen families on our church roll now. I would love it but doubling our church membership in two years is setting a very high goal."

Hazel spoke up. "Yes, that would be a revival!"

Clarice asked Bro. Mike, "Do you think you need to change our music, remodel our sanctuary, or get some of those new screens?"

"Those decisions will be up to your preference but are not required by this approach. Please keep mind that most of the people we will be reaching have not been to a church in years. They are not church shoppers. They generally are not comparing your worship services with those of other churches. The most important factors will be the Lord's leading and relationships. In fact, outside the Spirit leading you and them, showing them the love of Christ through relationships will be key."

Rose King spoke up saying, "Bro. Mike, before we conclude, I have one more question if it is okay."

"Sure," said Mike.

"Where do you think we might find these two people? We are all older and most of our friends are older."

Mike said, "Like I said, every step begins and ends with prayer. For us it is a long shot, but not for God. I think God has already prepared two people for this purpose. It is just a matter of you all finding who they are."

Bro. Norman said, "Thank you, Brother Mike. We will work through the pre- and post-test and see you again next Wednesday week at 6:30, if the Lord is willing."

Bro. Mike signed off the conference call.

"Well, I just don't know," said Rose. "Who would want to help us part-time for $150 per week, knowing they had to at least reach five families in a year for our church? This sounds like we are giving a bounty for lost people."

Everyone laughed.

Bro. Norman said, "I do not think that is what Mike meant at all. However, I think accountability and expectations are important. Think about it; we did the same with Sunday School goals all through the years. We know it is not about the numbers, it is about the souls."

After working through all the questions scanning the pages, Will closed the session in prayer. Everyone understood the assignment was praying for two people to serve as church missionaries. Bro. Norman said, "Remember God's word tells us we have not because we ask not."

Brent Lay

14

"Follow Me"

Bro. Norman felt led to bring a message about the calling of the disciples the next Sunday. After the greeting time, he asked all to pray for the two people who could serve their church as part-time church missionaries. He said copies of the ministry description could be found on the table in the foyer.

The morning message focused upon how each of disciples responded to the call of Jesus. Bro. Norman pointed out that those men were accessible, adaptable, and persistent.

"Obviously," Bro. Norman alluded, "these men had faith relationships with the Father already. They had a history of listening to God."

He continued, "Whoever the Lord has for us to serve in our church missionary positions, I feel they will have a history of listening to God. They will take His call to heart because they already walk with the Lord and are accessible." He described it as putting their *yes* on the table to whatever God was asking of them.

"Secondly," Bro. Norman said, "our future church missionaries will be adaptable. The disciples gave up their profession of fishing to become fishers of men. This meant a new way of life, an entirely new direction."

Bro. Norman continued. "Thirdly, whoever Jesus calls to serve at our church will be someone who will not look back after putting his or her hand to the plow."

He reminded everyone that outreach and evangelism are some of the most challenging ministries of the church. He shared his own experiences over the years of sharing the Gospel and sharing his life with strangers when not many responded. He described the first disciples as fishermen who knew what it was to keep fishing when they were not catching fish. In fact, he said with a smile, "I determined that is why we say fishermen, because good fishermen keep fishing even when the fish are not biting. This is something I never had the patience to do personally when fishing."

He continued and repeated, "The two people God will call to serve us will be like the disciples. They will be accessible to the call, adaptable, and persistent with their ministry, helping connect others with our church."

He concluded asking all to pray diligently each day and he asked each person to call at least five family members or friends and ask them to join them in this specific prayer.

15

Hallelujah! Oh My!

The next Wednesday night, the meeting involved all sorts of emotions. Even as others arrived, several of the ladies said they could hardly sleep at night thinking about what God was doing. But other members of the team seemed to be shaking their head expressing doubts of finding people to serve.

Bro. Norman, after an opening prayer, said, "I have prayed and thought for hours already as to who they could be, and I have not had one person come to mind." He continued, "But I know God is able."

Mildred shared that she had asked seven other people to join her in prayer for God's two people.

"Yep," Will shared, "I was afraid there was a catch to this whole idea. I am thinking we have been led down a rabbit's hole, and an empty one at that. I was thinking this morning, we must be off our rockers. Think about it, we can barely afford a part-time pastor, a part-time minister of music, a nursery worker, and a part-time janitor."

Gordon, Jr., who worked at a local bank for several years as a clerk, joined the conversation. "Since I have been a member here, we have had three full-time pastors and some of those other positions were filled at times, yet we decreased in attendance almost every year. It seems to me we do not have choice but try another way."

Earline said, "Let's not get discouraged, Will. I think this is going to work and I know someone that I think will do it. It is my granddaughter, Shelby. She is going to college about 55 miles from here. I always thought of her as a missionary. She hands out tracts and witnesses to other students all the time. She could come spend the night with me two or three nights a week, including most weekends. Besides that, the Lord knows she could use the money."

"Let us all put her name on our prayer list," responded Bro. Norman. "She is really young to be doing this, but God works in mysterious ways."

Clarice said, "The Lord has laid it on my heart that we should consider you, Hazel. You know our church and the community well. Besides that, your stipend would be more than the $50 per week we were paying you. So, we all could have your cake and you could eat it, too, with your new teeth!"

Everyone looked at Hazel and smiled awaiting a response.

Hazel said, "I appreciate your thought, but I do not feel I am the person. I do not hear well on the phone anymore and I rarely drive at night. I think whoever these people are, they are going to have to go out and visit from time to time."

Herman said, "Bro. Norman, Will does have a point. Do you think we might be able to find a fellow who could serve as our pastor and do all this connection ministry also?"

Bro. Norman said, "I thought about that weeks ago. I even discussed it with Bro. Mike. I was thinking maybe some young whipper-snapper preacher might be the very thing. Bro. Mike reminded me that over these many years, it averaged out involving 70 to 80 hours of interaction with a prospect before they became members. After I thought about it, I think that amount of time is about right. It explains why even the most outreach-driven pastor has a limit as to how many families will be reached each year as far as joining the church."

Mike added, "In terms of building relationships, which is key, the pastor only has one or two nights each week that he can dedicate for outreach efforts. These part-time people as church missionaries have the same number of Tuesday and Friday nights as the pastor, so it really does multiply the hours invested in outreach ministry. The pastor usually becomes the closer, so to speak, since he is involved after relationships with the prospects and church members have been built. This saves an enormous amount of time for the pastor. The pastor becomes more efficient in terms of outreach which allows the pastor more time for study and for his family."

As the others listened intently, Bro. Norman continued. "Being a pastor all these years and as one who attended seminary to be a preacher, I tell you that most of us pastors really like to spend most of our time preparing to preach. I will speak for myself. I do not see my strength as some sort of strategist or a trained change agent. And, honestly, I think most preachers are like me. We feel primarily called to preach the Word. This connection ministry material has convinced me that it really is a missionary strategy. I often think of Author Flake, that businessman from Mississippi who eventually led our Sunday School emphasis throughout the Southern Baptist Convention. He was the fellow who came up with the formula known as Flake's formula. That was a wonderful tool the Lord blessed, resulting in tremendous growth for most Southern Baptist Churches. My point is, he was not a preacher. As God's Word tells us, we each have different spiritual gifts."

Gordon, Jr., responded, "I know very little about the preaching ministry or what it takes to be a pastor, but I totally agree. Bro. Bill had us spend $3,000 to send out those jumbo postcards after he came. He was convinced that when everyone in Bacon County knew he was here as our new preacher, they would come hear him preach and we would overflow with people. Best I remember, we had less than ten new people visit over the next few weeks and none of them came back after hearing him preach. I have come to realize that most folks in our area are not looking for the best preaching or a church. The lost folks are not going to get saved at our church if they are not here. We definitely are going to have to get involved with them out there."

Herman said, "Now that you say that, Gordon, I think you all remember that I volunteered to do the cassette tape ministry for Bro. Dawson twenty years ago. I put 8 to 10 tapes at 10 different places for months and he told me that he got some letters and calls, but as far as I know, no one came to our church as result. Our church even sponsored for him to be on the radio twice each week, but I do not recall anyone new coming to our church because they heard him on the radio. I enjoyed listening to him and it was a gift to our community but as far as I know, it did not grow our church."

"Fellows," said Bro. Norman, "you are right. Those efforts, for the most part, have not worked in recent years. You said a lot, Gordon, when you said folks are not looking for a church these days. I find that in my own witnessing, I refrain from talking about our church or church programs and focus instead upon building a relationship. I find folks are hungry for relationships. Sharing and showing the love of Christ has worked well all my life. In the old days of Sunday School, we always described this relationship building as cultivating."

"Now you are singing my song," said Gordon, Jr. "I can tell you; I did not come to this church for the preaching, music, or programs. I came because friends had reached out to me and I was saved. I wanted to be baptized in a church."

Everyone smiled. Gordon, Jr., worked at the Peoples Bank downtown. He had been assigned vault duty, as he called it, for several weeks. His job was to monitor the deposits and withdrawals from the bank vault, which was situated in the basement. As it turned out, he had a few hours in the middle of each day that passed very slowly, and he had time to read books. Susan, one of the ladies upstairs, told him she had a series of books he must read. They were the *Left Behind* book series by Tim LaHaye and Jerry Jenkins. Within a week, he was asking his friend Susan all about being a Christian. One day, as he was alone in the basement, he prayed for the Lord to save his soul.

Sadie Hadley, his mother, had been coming to Stump Creek for more than twenty years with her two grown daughters until they moved away. Gordon, Jr., brought his wife Pam and their daughter Katie on a Sunday morning to the surprise of his mother. He came to profess his faith, be baptized, and join the church, just as his friend Susan had explained.

The funny part of his story that morning was he

did not know one had to wait until the end of the service. He got there early and told the preacher what happened and said, "I am ready to come forward right now." The preacher told him, "We are going to have some singing and then some preaching and then you can come." Gordon, Jr., told him, "I don't know if I can wait that long. How long does that last?" Gordon, Jr., had shared his testimony many times and always added that was the longest sermon he had ever heard in his entire life.

Everyone remembered that occasion because what Gordon, Jr., did not know was that his dad, Gordon, Sr., at 75 years old, had prayed to receive Christ himself. The very next Sunday after Gordon, Jr., came forward, his wife Pam also came, and two weeks later, all three stood in the baptistry together. All three were baptized that morning. That was the last time multiple baptisms had taken place.

"Oh, my," said Hazel, "it would be such a shame for us not to find the two people God is calling to serve in this ministry."

"Oh-my is my thinking, too," said Will. "We definitely have experienced a hallelujah time. I never dreamed we would have the money to try this new idea and I am so thankful for all of you and what God has done. It truly is *oh-my* time. We have done got ourselves out on a limb. I mean a long limb."

Rose said, "We're just going to have to keep on praying."

Bro. Herman closed the meeting in prayer telling the Lord, "We really don't know how to go about this, we have not been down this path before. We have stepped out in faith. Lord, we know we are out on a limb. Whoever the people are, Lord, that You have for us, let them know and us know. In Your holy name, we pray. Amen."

16

Prospects Verses Suspects

Two weeks passed and all team members gathered with Bro. Norman. He borrowed his grandson's smart phone so they could again talk and see Bro. Mike the same as before.

Bro. Norman started the meeting saying, "Hello, Bro. Mike, we all are here. I am going to turn the meeting over to you."

"Great," said Bro. Mike. "Tonight's session by design is to talk about the all-important task of prospecting. I have you on my prayer list and hopefully within the next few weeks, it will become clear who God is calling to serve your church as church missionaries or connection coordinators, depending on the name you choose."

Herman spoke up. "Bro. Mike, if I can interrupt you, are you saying we continue to do some preliminary work even though we don't even know if we are going to find people to do this?"

"Yes," answered Mike, "Bro. Herman, it usually takes several weeks to bring a person online as your first church missionary. Tonight's session about prospecting is a task that you as the church missionary team will need to do anyway. In a worst-case scenario, the process of prospecting and the next session of planning invite events will enhance your possibilities of growth. Both of these sessions include practices that involved 27 years of trial and error to determine the approaches that usually work best."

"First," said Bro. Mike, "let me remind you all again that this is a spiritual endeavor. We continually pray as we seek to experience God and know His will at every turn. Please keep this in mind as I do not want the spiritual nature of this ministry to be overlooked as we talk about the mechanics of how this ministry works. With that said," continued Mike, "we need to discover many prospects even before the church missionaries begin."

"How many do you suggest?" asked Gordon, Jr.

Mike replied, "Since we are planning for two church missionaries, we need to pray and think about as many as 100 family units."

"Woo-wee!" said Earline out loud and everyone laughed.

"What do you mean by family units?" asked Gordon.

Mike answered, "We count single-person homes as family units, just like families of five or more. We have found that we usually reach one family unit at a time. For an example, over the years, you all had children reached through Vacation Bible School that eventually led to their parents coming to your church also."

Gordon reiterated, "So what you are saying is 100 family units could represent 300 to 400 more people."

Before Bro. Mike could answer, Herman interrupted. "Bro. Mike, I think you have got us mixed up with some other church. We never had more than five hundred members at any one time. Why would we need to be thinking about such an outrageous amount? It could take us five years to come up with 100 families."

Bro. Mike laughingly said, "Well, you folks are awake tonight! In all seriousness, it takes a lot of prospects because there are a lot of reasons newly saved folks will end up joining another church. Sometimes it happens because they have family or close friends at another area church. Other times, because of their background, they feel more comfortable attending a church of another denomination. It will not be unusual to invest a year or so of connection ministry with families or individuals who end up joining another church. But we are in the Kingdom business first and foremost, so we never regret our witnessing and connecting with others, as long as they are active in another church."

"Perhaps your church used Evangelism

Explosion, Continued Witness Training, or the FAITH strategy over the years. During those years, many churches were reaching out and seeing people saved, but in many cases only about one out of ten of those newly saved people actually joined their church. Some churches were seeing folks saved but continued in decline."

Will spoke up. "Bro. Mike, we can come up with lots of names of folks who do not go to church if that is what you are asking. I am a surveyor by trade and we have four or five subdivisions being developed within five miles of our church. I can put together a list of those who have moved into our area in a matter of a couple of weeks. I think I could give you a list of at least 50 families, or family units as you called them, who have moved into our area in the last two years."

"That is good start, Will," replied Mike. "A list of 50 family units sounds great. That list will help lead us to our goal which is prospects. Our end goal is to discover prospects, not just suspects. Prospects are those we have reason to believe are lost and in need of a church. They are those we already know something about through friends, family, co-workers, neighbors, or our own personal interaction. We have a saying that goes, the better we know them, the better we serve them. Just to have names and addresses is what we fondly refer to as suspects. We hope and pray that every last one of the suspects will turn out to be a bona fide prospect. The idea is we need a list of people that we know information about and feel led to invest lots of time building relationships with them. Naturally, each missionary can only focus upon connecting or building bridges with only 8 to 10 at a time. This strategic focus adjusting each week is key."

Bro. Mike continued, "We will go into great detail with your church missionaries about this process as they generally will focus on no more than ten families at a time. As the church missionaries continue week to week, they will average spending about an hour or more with each family each week. Some weeks might involve five hours or so interaction with one family, but it will average out about an hour per week for each family for twelve or more months."

Mike continued, "It is important we actually have names and details on our list. First, this list we refer to as our outreach log, also represents your prayer list. It is amazing as you pray for say, Joel and his family members by name every day, how the Lord will put that family in your path. Even though the church missionary will be doing most of the personal interaction, you as the team will be the prayer warriors and facilitators to assist and support the church missionary. Your role as a support team is very important. Your primary tasks once the church missionaries are aboard will include praying, prospecting, and planning, as well as facilitating invite events."

"So, your goal is to discover and list 100 families in the area, with details about that family, including the general age bracket of the adults and children. You will be surprised how many parents will say they can attend almost any church as long as their child has friends there. Connecting friends is one way of describing this ministry. One of our themes is finding friends forever. As relationships are built and people become followers of Christ, they will truly be our friends forever in Heaven."

Mike continued explaining, "It is also a matter of timing. It has been our experience, that out of 50 family units, only 10 or so of those families will be our best prospects at any given time. Again, God is at work. Sometimes things happen with families including getting good news or bad news, that provides us a window of opportunity to connect with them and minister to them. As the result of prayer, you will be surprised how the Lord will prompt you to reach out to them at the very best time. One of the most common responses from people sometimes is, *how did you know*? These life-changing events include things like graduations, job loss, death, marriages, health crisis, financial crisis and even divorce. We are not discounting or deleting any people from our prospect list, but through God's guidance, we love to find those divine appointments."

Clarice said, "I know this is a dumb question, but how are we going to find out all this information about all these new people?"

"Great question," said Bro. Mike. "You all probably remember the book entitled *Concentric Circles of Concern* by W. Oscar Thompson, Jr. The thinking in that book is we all have a certain amount of influence and knowledge of people in circles around us. You each have unchurched neighbors. You may have unchurched family members. You probably have unchurched folks that work on your vehicles and your houses. Other circles may include folks that we see regularly out and about like at the grocery store or beauty shop. As we seek to have the Father's eyes, the Lord seems to reveal to us lost people that we already know something about."

"The extreme advantage of this approach is that many names that go on your prospect list are people your people already know. You may not even remember their name, but you or another member of your church has known them for years. As you help put together this outreach log, the details about each family unit reveals to us connection points. If you already know they work at the hospital, have a boat, and have two daughters who are five and seven years old, all of those details represent very valuable information. Most importantly, if a church member knows them and they know that church member, your church member may be in the best position to begin the connection process. The church missionary is coordinating all of this connection activity every week, so in effect, you are maximizing all your people's capacity to reach others. Instead of having two hours per week of an outreach effort as a church, you are putting into motion 50 to 100 hours per week without the pastor having to lead and do most of it."

Mike continued, "Connection points are like the *Lego* toys; those details give us insight as what a member of your church may have in common with them and makes for a good fit. Say, you have an acquaintance with a fellow at the barber shop. You already know enough to know he does not go to church, but you also know he is an avid golfer. Perhaps, he brings it up in conversations all the time. Well, guess what? You probably have someone in your church, or you have a grandson or a good friend who also plays golf, and so that detail of information leads us to a possible connection point."

"So, here is the assignment: begin praying and making a list of people who you think are most likely unchurched and you know some information about. When I say unchurched, I include folks not active in a church. Since there are nine of you there tonight, if each of you come up with five, we are on our way as that will be 45 of our 100 goal."

Bro. Norman interjected, "Well, Bro. Mike, I think we understand the assignment and since it is getting late, we will sign off for now. We will visit with you Wednesday week at 6:30. Thank you."

Mike replied, "Good night."

Will spoke up immediately, saying, "I tell you, the more I hear about this ministry, the steeper this hill becomes. If we knew 100 families that were prospects to attend our church, we could surely reach some of them without having to hire any part-time people."

"You may be right, Will, but I recommend we stay the course for now. Let's see what God has in store," said Bro. Norman. "Let us pray for God's call on two people and for this list of 100 bona fide prospects. In the meantime, if anyone has a lead on a person that could serve, I will be glad to do some follow-up."

Gordon, Jr., was asked to close in prayer. He included in his prayer, "we are not seeing too far ahead right now, Lord, but we know that is why we call it faith. We have faith, Lord, that You will continue to lead us in our weakness."

Brent Lay

17

"Answered Prayers"

By the next Wednesday evening, word had got around that Rose King had a recommendation to make concerning a possible candidate to serve. She had contacted Bro. Norman the week before and asked two or three of the ladies to join her in praying for Wanda Barnette. Wanda Barnette and her husband Russ were originally from the area but had relocated more than 20 years earlier to Indiana for Russ to work at a corporate office. Russ was taking an early retirement. They were very active members of their small church in Indiana. Russ had served as the chairman of deacons on several occasions and Wanda had been involved with every aspect of the church, including leading the children's ministry.

Rose exclaimed in talking to the group, "You are not going to believe how this happened. I was having coffee with my neighbor Sherry who attends First Baptist, and I was asking her to pray with me that we might find someone to serve. Within five minutes, she told me about some friends that had stayed with her just two weeks before and were moving here soon. She called Wanda while I was there and asked if she would consider serving in a part-time outreach role at a nearby Baptist church. She told Sherry she would like to hear more about it and Sherry arranged for me to call her back that afternoon at three o'clock. I called Wanda and read the ministry description to her and she seemed to be taking notes. She sounded very interested and said she and her husband had been talking about getting involved in some volunteer missions work." Rose started crying, saying, "It seems like God has been laying something like this on Wanda's heart for years. I called Bro. Norman and he has talked to Wanda also."

"Yes, Wanda is a good candidate, I would say," chimed in Bro. Norman. "She has lots of questions and of course, she and her husband need time to pray about it. I found out that she and her husband attended a wedding years ago at our church. They are moving into a new house about four miles away this Friday and will be very busy. At this juncture, the most important thing for us to do is pray, and if the Lord leads her and us in the same direction, I will set up a time for all of you to meet her."

"In the meantime," Bro. Norman continued, "We have more news. Herman, would you like to go next?"

"Sure," said Herman. "I think I know another candidate. Most of you might know Ray Barnes and his wife Ruth. They are long-time members at First Baptist (one of the larger churches in the area about 12 miles away, which had relocated at the intersection of two major highways). Ole Ray has been a good friend of mine for years. In fact, he sold me some life insurance years ago. He just retired from selling insurance at 67 years old."

Herman continued, "I ran into him at the grocery store and asked him to pray for us, that we were considering doing something new at our church. When I told Ray that it involved a part-time missionary position, he said, 'as a matter of fact, I might be interested.' I was speechless and just stared at him. Finally, I told him 'you've got to be kidding.' I told him I thought he said he had just retired. Ray then told me he had, but he felt the Lord had more for him to do. He shared that his wife Ruth knew he always had to be on a mission and liked to stay busy. Ray already knows we have a challenging situation at Stump Creek. He told me he liked a challenge even when he played golf."

"I told Ray that I would bring him some information so he and Ruth could pray about the possibility. That was last Thursday, and on Friday morning he called me and said he would like to talk more. He told me that moving his membership might be a deal-breaker because they have been members at First Baptist for 31 years. Ruth loves her Sunday School class and does not want to give it up. But Ray did say he and Ruth could go to the 8 o'clock service at First and he could be at our church for our Sunday School at 9:30. I told him I would bring up his name with our team and I would get back with him."

By this point, the ladies were looking at each other and tearing up. Will and Gordon were looking at each other with slight smiles and raised eyebrows.

Brother Norman said, "We have a lot to pray about. With your permission, I will continue to exchange information with Wanda and Ray. Hopefully, all of us, including Wanda and Ray, will find God's will."

Bro. Norman continued, "I have one other item of news to report. I received a call yesterday from Dr. Ricky Smith who does dental implants. He said he had a friend from his church who called saying he had heard about what Hazel Everett had done for her church."

About that time, the ladies were crying with some lifting their hands. Hazel bent over in her chair with her head in her hands. The other fellows were all looking away, like they were looking out the window.

Bro. Norman continued, "Dr. Smith told me he would provide the dental implants for Hazel for free because his friend was going to pay for them."

Hazel, as she wept, blurted out that Dr. Smith

was her dentist.

Bro. Norman responded, "I figured so, but I suppose he felt he could not tell me that."

Mildred, sitting next to Hazel, was the first to hug her, saying, "Oh, Hazel we love you." All the ladies stood and encircled Hazel, taking turns hugging as all continued to weep with joy. Then a strange but beautiful silence seemed to fill the room.

Gordon, Jr., broke the silence saying, "If it's okay with everyone, I would like to lead us in a little chorus that is one of my favorites."

Bro. Norman said, "That would be swell, Gordon. Let's make this our benediction. We will meet again next Wednesday." And everyone stood. Gordon led, and everyone sung along this little chorus:

Nothing is impossible when you put your trust in God,

Nothing is impossible when you're trusting in His Word,

Harken to the voice of God to thee, is there anything too hard for me?

Then put your trust in God alone and rest upon His Word,

Yes, everything, Yes, everything, everything is possible with God.

(Composer Eugene Clark, 1925-1982, copyright 1966)

As they were walking out the door, Bro. Norman told Gordon, Jr., that he really liked that little chorus. He asked him to plan for the congregation to sing it at the Sunday worship services for the next few weeks.

18

Widow of Zarephath

It was the first Sunday in March. Twenty-six were in attendance, which was more than twice the attendance just a few weeks before. One or two had neighbors to come, and Liz's daughter's family was there, as well as Earline's son's family of four. It was great seeing children sitting on those dark, red-cushioned wooden pews. The singing of the *Nothing is Impossible* chorus was very moving. The team members made a point to smile at each other as they sang out with abiding joy.

Bro. Norman introduced his sermon about Elijah and the Widow at Zarephath, from I Kings 17:7-16. As Brother Norman began, he shared that he had a really good week and felt the Lord was stirring his heart. He said, "You know I have been doing this pastoring for a long time and only a few times have I felt the stirring of the Spirit as I have this week. Your church missionary team and I have seen signs of God answering prayers. Please continue to pray diligently."

The theme of the sermon was, "the process of faith is sometimes as important as the product of faith." The point he continued to make was that God used the little handful of flour and the little amount of olive oil in a big way because the widow had trusted, giving up her very last meal.

He said, "God owns all the cattle and the hills they are on. He does not need your money. He does not need my money. God did not need that little handful of flour, nor the last drops of the widow's olive oil. God was testing her faith. Through her faith, much was added. So, it is with our life journey."

Bro. Norman continued, "Looking back, most of us will not remember what we gave, but we will remember trusting the Lord. And we know the Lord will remember us. The process of faith is much like what God's Word says in Malachi 3:10, *Put me to the test, saith the Lord of hosts*."

Concluded Bro. Norman, "Like the song we sing, *Trust Me, Try Me and Prove Me*, may we be found trusting, and may we experience the proving of the Lord."

19

"Too Much Work!"

Sunday afternoon lunch at Rose King's was delightful as usual. What was unusual was how quiet Herman and Clarice were. Finally, as they were about to partake of the lemon icebox pie, Bro. Norman asked Herman, "Are you okay? You don't seem yourself today."

"Well," said Herman, "as a matter of fact, I have got some bad news for you."

"What is that?" ask Bro. Norman.

"Clarice and I are not in the best of health and have been consumed with this church missionary business for almost two months now. She and I have prayed, studied, and talked about it so much that we are wore out. The bottom line, Bro. Norman, is we have decided that we need to get off that church missionary team. It is just too much work for old folks like us."

Bro. Norman said, "Ah, Herman, we are about to get over the hardest part, thanks to your leadership and your help in interacting with Ray."

"Well," said Herman, "that is what I thought when the Lord worked out all the money. But this

91

stuff about prospects and invite events, it is like doing a job. We like just going to church and not having to worry about all that stuff. We love the fellowship, our Sunday School classes, and our church services. I can see why some people don't want to get involved in this church missionary stuff because it simply absorbs your life."

"Herman," replied Bro. Norman in a very tender way, "you have almost said verbatim what Bro. Mike told me weeks ago. He said the top two questions folks ask on the front end is why not use all volunteers and is not this ministry something that all the members need to be doing anyway. Mike explained that in the beginning when this strategy was started, they tried to use only volunteers. But within weeks, almost all the volunteers wanted to take a break. Most of the volunteers realized they did not want to spend so much time dealing with strangers on a regular basis. They found that most volunteers would give two hours or so per week doing visitation or writing letters and making calls. But they found that volunteers generally do not want to be responsible to give all the hours required week after week to connect folks on the outside of the church with the folks on the inside of the church."

Herman said, "I wonder if they tried rotating volunteers like doing the ministry for a couple of months and taking two months off. Clarice and I might consider something like that serving on the church missionary team."

Rose, sitting at the table and listening, chimed in. "That sounds like a possible solution. The last few weeks have been pretty intense. Don't get me wrong, they have been wonderful. But I sure like the sound of meeting only twice per month and let us be in a support role. I did not realize we would have homework assignments every week!"

They all laughed, and Bro. Norman replied, "It has been an intense month or so. I have found myself thinking how I got lassoed into a two-year commitment. I never intended to do that."

Bro. Norman continued, "I tell you what, I will suggest that as soon as we get the two missionaries in place that we as an entire team meet on the first Tuesday of each month, and maybe half of us meet another Tuesday so that would be three accountability meetings for the church missionaries each month. I recall Mike saying that having at least three of these meetings per month was necessary. He said it helped keep the accountability and also helped coordinate interactions between church members and prospects. As a favor, I ask you all hang in there. We are very close to getting Wanda and Ray aboard. I think at some point soon, they will do the heavy lifting and we will be in that support role."

"I hope so," said Herman. "I sure would like to

get my nap times in again," he said as he started rubbing his head. "I hope Wanda and Ray work out. We really will need to support them in a big way. If they feel half the pressure Clarice and I have felt this last month, they face a huge challenge. If I had to keep up with ten prospective families at a time, trying to make all these connections, and report back to a team of members every week, I doubt if I could sleep at all!"

20

Explaining Invite Events

"Bro. Mike, we are all here except Mildred, as she had a trip planned this week. The rest of us are raring to go," said Bro. Norman as the phone conference began. "I have told the team that you and I visited on the phone about what happened last week and that you know about the possibility of Wanda and Ray coming aboard."

"Wonderful news," said Mike. "I will continue to pray that it will be a fit for both those candidates. And congratulations, Hazel. Your story inspires us all. God bless you!"

"He has!" replied Hazel.

"Tonight," said Mike, "is our last scheduled session with you as a team. I will have a session or so with your church missionaries whenever they come aboard. As I said last week, the invite events, like the prospecting, is something we need for you as a team to begin even before we have missionaries in place. An invite event, by our definition, is any event or occasion that affords you an opportunity to invite a prospect to interact with you and other church members."

"By the way, how are you doing with making your list of prospects?"

"I have four," said Gordon, Jr.

Earline spoke up and said she had four also.

"Does everyone have at least have two?" Mike asked.

Herman spoke up. "I think everyone has at least two except Clarice and I. I spent so much time talking to Ray and carrying him material to read, the last two weeks just got by too fast."

"I understand," said Bro. Mike. "You see these meetings are necessary because we all have unexpected interruptions. For most of us, we have a tendency to do what we know we will be accountable for. It is human nature. That is why I strongly encourage you to make sure you have weekly sessions with your church missionaries. Hazel, if you do not mind, I will ask everyone to pass along their prospect information to you by the end of this meeting so you might make the master list like the example of the outreach log in the material. From this time forward, all of you please forward any prospects information to Hazel."

Mike continued, "Would anyone share how they discovered two or more prospects from the same source."

Rose spoke up and said, "I was praying about this the other morning and remembered seeing a moving truck pass by my house headed into the new subdivision nearby. I drove down there and found a lady out in her front yard. She attends church over at Freshwater, but told me the names of three new neighbors, one whom just moved in this last week. She thought one of the families had a Baptist background. She knew something about all of them, including the age of their children and where they worked. I am thinking I am going to deliver some brownies to each of those homes soon to find out more."

"There you go," said Bro. Mike. "Like we talked about last week, what Rose has at this point are suspects, but as soon as she has a few door visits, she will have a good idea if any are actually as we say *bona fide prospects*. Folks moving into homes are sometimes just relocating within the area and are faithful at another church. Remember though that every lead on suspects is valuable because they usually lead us to good prospects."

Bro. Mike referenced the handouts about invite events and pointed out that there were two main categories: the piggyback and the designed purposed. The piggyback category involves enhancing almost every event that the church does anyway as an opportunity to invite a guest. Mike shared that the reason invite events were so important is because you usually can only invite folks to attend your church once or twice.

Mike said, "After that, many will shun you as

they feel that you are badgering them. Sometimes they begin to think that the primary reason you want them is for nickels and noses. Outsiders sometimes think it is really not about them personally at all. Instead, they think that you reaching out to them is really about keeping your bills paid."

"In practice, we have found that the same folks who will be turned off by inviting them to church continually are very open to you continually inviting them to events that they perceive will be enjoyable. And, they sense that you are reaching out because you genuinely desire to be their friend. For example, has your church ever had a fish fry or a chili cook-off?"

Earline spoke up and said, "We have done both years ago, but it was for the members, not guests."

Mike replied, "Suppose you had a chili supper for the members but enhanced the occasion to invite guests. Say you print up tickets with a tear-off stub that might even have $8 per meal cost on them. The members could buy tickets, but also receive five or more free tickets to give to guests. By asking for the stubs, you would have a reservation list. On the ticket, you do not want to mention just any old chili cook-off; you highlight that your event includes homemade desserts and homemade ice cream. In practice, we call this the 'selling of the sizzle.'"

Several laughed at that.

"So, Gordon, what do you think you will talk

about when you ask an unchurched friend about being your guest?"

Gordon replied, "I would be sure to mention the home-made ice cream!"

"To make it even more inviting, you might share that you are bringing your famous homemade peach ice cream," added Mike.

Mike continued to share. "Now, for an example of a designed purpose invite event. A few years back, some ladies that came up with the idea of a Christmas home tour involving five decorated homes which turned out to be a five-course progressive meal starting at 4 p.m. on a Saturday afternoon. By design, it was only for a few church members who pitched in to provide the food, promote the event, and provide childcare. The first stop was a home which had a nice recreation room in a walk-out basement that was perfect for childcare. Two college students were hired to provide the childcare, and that was called a children's party. Fourteen prospective couples from the sixty invited prospective families made reservations. Think about that; fourteen unchurched couples mixing with church people all afternoon, having a great time and enjoying wonderful hospitality and food. They as a church were truly putting their best foot forward with this carefully designed invite event. Two of the guest families showed up the very next day at their church. Over the next year, three new families joined their church who had attended that event."

Mike continued, "By using these invite events, we are conveying that we truly care about others and value our relationship with them. It is sharing the love of Christ. Over time with these people, we will have the opportunities to share our faith. Usually, most of these new friends will eventually try out your church as they feel led. And of those who try out your church, there will be some who will accept Christ as their personal Savior and eventually join your church. As we all know, only God gives the increase."

"You have the material in front of you with a calendar for the next six months," Mike continued. "Your assignment is to discuss and plan at least one invite event for each month of the next six months, which is primarily for the purpose of outreach. Be sure to have at least one third of the events away from the church property. This is because many of our prospects have had bad experiences with churches and are suspicious of what is going to happen when they come to your church for any event. When they feel completely relaxed, knowing the agenda is having fun and sharing time together, they are more likely to accept your invitation. Of course, pray every step of the way!"

Then Mike said, "Let me conclude by saying again that praying, prospecting, and planning, as well facilitating invite events, are the major functions that you as a team will need to do over the months ahead. If you do these well, you will be setting each of your church missionaries up to succeed, reaching at least five family units per year. Just think, your devotion to this outreach is going to lead to ten or more new family units attending your church within eighteen months. For your size church, if the new families come at least half the time as they normally do, your church is going to double in attendance within the next eighteen months."

"Bro. Norman, I will turn it back over to you. Thank you everyone, and may God give the increase!" said Mike as he concluded.

Bro. Norman said, "I have some good news to share. Wanda and Ray have agreed to come next Tuesday evening. We will interview Wanda at 6:30 and Ray at 7:45. Please continue to pray for these folks and our task between now and then."

Bro. Norman asked Herman to conclude the meeting in prayer.

Brent Lay

21

"Never Like This Again"

The next Tuesday night seemed to come fast. Bro. Norman's message on the Sunday before was about the importance of adapting to win the more. His text included the testimony of Apostle Paul that "he became all things to all people that by all means he might save some."

All the team members were able to attend the meeting to interview Wanda and Ray, and all arrived early. Wanda seemed very familiar. Her husband Russ also came and quietly took a seat in the corner of the room. She had talked extensively to Rose and Bro. Norman. After she was introduced, she said most of her questions had been answered and that she and her husband Russ had prayed about it. She said she would commit to giving it her best try. The paperwork said either party could terminate the employment with three weeks' notice, no questions asked.

One of the first questions was for her to describe her church work in recent years. She related that they loved their church in Libertyville, Indiana. Russ had been a deacon the entire twenty-one years there and had led the pastor search committee twice. She described how she led the children's ministry when her son was young and later the youth ministry. She and Russ had always participated in church visitation programs. Being one of the few Southern Baptist churches in the area, she described the difficulty growing the church as the church stayed about the same size. At one point, she had served as the church secretary.

Another line of questioning concerned her personal testimony, and did she believe that every person could be saved. She related how she grew up in a church about 30 miles south of Stump Creek and surrendered her life to Christ at age nine. Wanda said, "If you are asking me if I believe in Calvinism or Reformed theology, I know what it is, and I believe literally what Scripture says, that whosoever calls upon the Lord shall be saved."

As the session grew to a close, Wanda said, "I want you to know I look forward to being paid for serving, but that is not why I am willing to do this. Russ and I had talked about making some mission trips in our retirement. We feel led to give more time doing kingdom work anyway. When Rose and I first talked, it just seemed to be a fit, as I had planned to work part-time after we moved here. And one more thing," she said, "I worked for the local Chamber for two years in Indiana as a Welcome Lady for newcomers to our county. The more I read about this ministry, I thought this is like being a welcome lady for the church."

After the thank you and prayer, she and Russ made their way out as they knew the team had another person to interview for another position that night.

Most of the team already knew Ray and Ruth and they were all smiles and hugs as the two were escorted into the room by Bro. Norman. Ray had been a deacon over the years and had participated in the Continued Witness Training and Faith evangelism program at First Baptist. He shared what he had told Herman about feeling like he needed a new challenge and something to do now that he was newly retired.

Will again asked a question along the lines of "do you believe people are regenerated prior to their prayer to receive Christ?"

Ray smiled and said, "No, I believe in a sinner's prayer. I have had the privilege to see several people saved in their homes when I was involved in visitation. I believe a person must believe upon the Lord Jesus Christ and repent of their sins before they are truly saved and made new."

Ray said he had read and studied all the material Herman had delivered. While it would be new to him, Ray said some of it was like what he always did in Sunday School, using the old Flake's Formula. He quickly quoted it: "One, know the possibilities. Two, enlarge the organization. Three, enlist and train the leaders. Four, provide the space. And five, go after the people!"

Arthur Flake, a lay person from Winona, Mississippi, became one of the first leaders in standardizing Sunday School at the Sunday School Board in 1920.

Ray followed-up with a smile. "There are some advantages to being old," he said. "Arthur Flake has always one of my heroes because he was a salesman by training, just like me."

Just as with Wanda's interview, everyone had a smile. Bro. Norman expressed the need to proceed after Ray's interview was over with the meeting for about fifteen minutes. Bro. Norman told the team members that they could pray over the matter for a few days and call him or pass along a note of their thoughts.

Bro. Herman said, "I make a motion right now that we go forward with each of them starting next week."

Bro. Norman clarified that Wanda and Russ planned to become members, but Ray and Ruth would still be members at First Baptist with Ray attending regularly and Fay attending just on occasions. Several nodded their head indicating that would be acceptable.

Will said, "I see now that this approach could work. I will go along if all of you want to go forward, but there is part of me that says no. I think this is going bring a lot of new people in here and they will want to take over this church. They will probably want to put those screens on the wall, have loud music, and replace our pews with chairs. I am just saying, maybe we need to think and pray about this one more time before we pull the trigger. Stump Creek will most likely never be the same church that we have all loved all these years. To be honest; I love our fellowship and our church like it has always been. Part of me just feels this way."

Gordon, Jr., quickly responded as he was seated next to Will. "Brother, I love and appreciate you, but the part of you that you just described as wanting to keep everything the same doesn't sound good to me. I probably would not even be here tonight if people did not make special efforts to reach out to me. You all made room for my mom and my dad, as well as me and my family. I know you love this church, and we all do, but things will not remain the same anyway and reaching others for Christ like me makes the difference for all eternity."

Liz added, "No one is going to grieve more than me if all those changes you mentioned take place. But I will be full of joy knowing we are being found faithful. I have a coffee mug at home someone gave me years ago that says on it, 'Let Go and Let God'. I think that is the mindset we have to keep. If we end up with that loud music, I will just cut off my hearing aids and smile. When we are all dead and gone, may this church still be reaching people."

"Amen," several echoed.

Bro. Norman said, "Thank you, Will, for being honest. It is only natural to hold on to what we have loved all these years. Just as I preached last Sunday, we must be willing to become all things to all people, that by all means some might be saved."

Will replied, "I know that for sure, Bro. Norman. I will second Herman's motion."

All voted in the affirmative.

Bro. Norman said, "Gordon, let us sing that little chorus once more. I think that is going to be our theme song for the next few months. Nothing is impossible when you put your trust in God."

22

"A Matter of Time"

Will was right. Many things at Stump Creek were never the same. Within weeks, the church had one of the most-attended Easter Egg Hunt events on a Saturday than ever before. More than 300 flyers and two large signs on the road helped bring 47 children to the fun time. Four prospective families were discovered.

On the reverse side of each of the flyers was a nice invitation to the Easter Service, and included a picture of family bibles to be gifted to each new family who came on Easter Sunday. Only four new families came, but Jim and Debbie Hanes were among them with their 14-year-old son, Aaron.

Jim came forward at the invitation telling Bro. Norman he wanted to be baptized. He explained that his grandmother carried him to church until he was about fourteen. He felt he was saved at a youth retreat but failed to be baptized. He promised his grandmother that someday he would be baptized, but she became ill and later died. The years passed and now Jim was 42 years old. Bro. Norman asked if he could visit him at his home on Monday night.

Upon arrival that night, Bro. Norman explained that he would be glad to baptize Jim, and he would like for him to consider church membership. Jim said that sounded fine to him if that was all right with Debbie. He looked at Debbie with a smile as she was seated next to him. Bro. Norman asked Debbie if she would consider joining also. She replied she did not know a lot about church and had never been in church before except for attending a Catholic Church with her friend when she was a teenager. Within a few minutes, Debbie and their son Aaron accepted Jesus as their personal Savior. All three were scheduled to be baptized the following Sunday.

Jim became the chief chair mover in the church since he was the most able-bodied and the older men bragged on him all the time. The very next week, Bro. Norman asked Aaron to help hand out bulletins at the entry door with Will. Aaron loved it and all the old folks loved him.

The blessings of the next seven months included 21 people joining the church and 7 baptisms. Wanda and Ray were working out fine. They each received about 20 hours of training through resources and consultations with Mike Sanders. Lives were being changed. Wanda and Ray made special efforts to ensure each new believer was discipled. All those reached considered Wanda or Ray as their best friend in the church. In many ways, they served as the gatekeepers and the disciple leaders for each new member. Included in this discipling was the process of finding a ministry for each new member.

Wanda gave leadership to having a Celebration Station for children on eight Wednesday evenings during the summer on the church lawn. It was promoted well with signs and handouts to more than 300 homes. Ray gave leadership to the grilling of free hamburgers and hotdogs.

Each Wednesday at 5 p.m. was an event of its own. A fire truck, National Guard vehicles, police cars, a police helicopter, a petting zoo, a water slide and jumpers were each featured on different Wednesday nights. The funny part was some of the parents and older members enjoyed such things as the petting zoo just as much as the children. Over those eight weeks, 52 children from 23 families participated. Seven of the families became good prospects. Three of the seven were single-mother parents.

On the second Sunday in October, Bro. Roger Stone came to visit the church. He greeted Bro. Norman after the service and asked to meet for lunch. They agreed that the following Thursday lunchtime would work.

At the luncheon, Bro. Roger began by saying, "Bro. Norman, I have to admit I was impressed with all I saw last Sunday. Praise the Lord for your leadership."

Bro. Norman with a smile said, "The Lord deserves all the glory. We have seen so many answered prayers. In all my years of serving as a pastor, the last seven months have been one of my best experiences. There is a sweet, sweet spirit with our people. Our people love the new people."

"Well, Norman," said Bro. Roger, "I suppose much of the growth is due to your fine preaching."

Bro. Norman laughed and said, "I am too old and now too humble to say that. You and I both know God gives the increase. Preaching the Word is central, but I cannot take the credit. Though years ago, I probably would have," he said laughingly.

"Do you think using that part-time missionary approach made the difference?" inquired Bro. Roger.

"Yes, even more than I imagined," said Bro. Norman. "Like Sunday School years ago, it is just another tool. But I can't tell you of a better tool for churches in today's world.

No disrespect, but over recent years it seems our convention and state conventions have followed a pattern of repeating a call for renewed goals, renewed focus, and renewed commitment about every seven to ten years. The obvious goal is to gain renewed enthusiasm for evangelism. I think it is very apparent that this repackaging the old methodologies with new names and slogans has not worked. On the other hand, this church missionary approach is entirely different and represents a fresh strategy.

The net result of getting a team of people within our church family focused on reaching others has been amazing. As things turned out in our case, we really are seeing far more effort from of our people. Most all our people will do anything and everything they can to help Wanda and Ray. In the old days, a guest would come and I would be one of few to even greet a guest. Now, when they see Wanda or Ray walking around with guests, our people are very careful to make each guest feel most welcomed. Most of our recent guests arrive already knowing several of our people because of all the connection ministry invite events. It's like old home week when our first-time guests arrive."

Bro. Norman continued, "You know Roger, building relationships is all about time. It is all about sharing the love of Christ. Sharing this love usually involves believers building relationships. I like to say, 'Love is spelled T I M E.' I think all of us as pastors have the best intentions and want to reach as many people as possible, but we only have so much time."

"That is an interesting observation," said Bro. Roger. "We have five or six other churches in our Association that are running less than forty on Sunday mornings and continue to decline."

"Yes, I am well aware," said Norman. "Most of those pastors are my friends and are good preachers. Ole codgers like me are always looking for preaching stations. That's what we do is preach. We were called to preach. We enjoy preaching and would do it even if there was no pay. Most pastors are like me and do not have the time or the energy to work every night of the week focused upon reaching people. In effect, because of Wanda's and Ray's use of our people, someone is interacting with prospects almost every night of the week. Stump Creek went from maybe two hours of outreach efforts each week to something like 50 hours each week. It has resulted in more than twenty times the effort in outreach than before, and I do not have to be in the middle of it. Most of it doesn't take place at the church and I get to gather the fruit once a week, for the most part, on Sundays."

"Wow," said Bro. Roger. "No wonder Stump Creek is growing."

Bro. Norman continued. "That is why I think this church missionary tool is going to be used more and more. I think when more pastors realize that it can save them so much time on outreach, they will be far more open to trying it. It is really nice preaching to new people and lost people for a change. Budgets are always tight with declining churches, so there is always reluctance to budget funds for something new. But once pastors and key leaders realize that this approach will eventually *grow* their budget and in turn grow the kingdom even more, I think they will want to do it. It really isn't going to cost them anything in the long run financially."

Bro. Roger said, "Yes, I saw on the website that the national goal is to see 400,000 church missionaries by the year 2034. I also remember seeing the *Million More by '34* slogan with the goal of a million more baptisms per year in our SBC convention of churches by the year 2034. Do you think that is a possibility?"

Bro. Norman replied with a smile. "Yes, I think it is very possible because this is a tool which will work at a church the size of Stump Creek or a church of thousands of members. We have to remember that the tool of Sunday School brought about similar dramatic growth in most of our churches back in the 1940's and 1950's. Twenty-five years ago, I would have not thought you and I would have phones which are computers in our pockets. I probably would have said I don't even want one. Who would want to be next to a phone all day every day? But here we sit. We cannot do without them."

"I think someday soon, that is what we will say about these church missionaries. We will say we cannot do without them. It is just a matter of time."

The End

About the Author

Dr. Brent Lay is a graduate of Union University (Tennessee), University of Memphis, Southern Baptist Theological Seminary (Kentucky), and Trinity Theological Seminary (Indiana). He holds two Master of Education degrees and a Doctor of Ministry degree. His 30-plus years of vocational ministry includes serving a director of missions, a minister of education and outreach, a headmaster at a Christian School, and as the Associate Pastor at Englewood Baptist Church, where he preached in the early worship service for seven years. During his tenure of twenty-five years on the staff at Englewood, the church more than tripled in attendance as well as the number of annual baptisms. It grew to be one of the largest churches in West Tennessee.

He is the founder and development director of the *Million More by '34,* national campaign aimed at Southern Baptists baptizing a million more each year beginning in 2034. This strategy is very similar in dynamics to the highly successful Apartment Life Coordinator ministry which has expanded exponentially to more than 30 states in recent years.

Brent is also the author of the book entitled: *Two-Part Romans (2PR), Resolving the Calvinism vs. Whosoever Will Puzzle!* (This book is available at Amazon Books.)

TENNESSEE BAPTISTS UNANIMOUSLY ADOPT RESOLUTION ENCOURAGING OUR SBC AND TBC LEADERSHIP AND ALL SBC CHURCHES!

November 11, 2015

WHEREAS, we are experiencing 50-year lows in the number of baptisms reported by Southern Baptist Churches nationwide; and

WHEREAS, the West Tennessee Innovative Evangelism Project previously supported by the Golden Offering for Tennessee Missions involves part-time church missionaries and has proven to be effective; and

WHEREAS, the development of this innovative strategy has involved six Tennessee Baptist churches during the past 27 years; and

WHEREAS, a grassroots movement is underway among Southern Baptist churches to deploy the strategy as described at the website millionmoreby34.com and this strategy is aligned with the Tennessee Baptist Convention's goal of 50,000 baptisms in Tennessee by 2024; and

WHEREAS, this strategy can be deployed by churches of any size as well as church plants.

NOW, THEREFORE, BE IT RESOLVED, that the messengers to the Tennessee Baptist Convention meeting in Millington, Tennessee on November 11, 2015, hereby encourage all Southern Baptist churches and our SBC and TBC leadership to support the implementation of this strategy and other appropriate strategies so that we as Tennessee Baptist may surpass our goal of 50,000 baptisms per year by 2024 and encourage Southern Baptists to baptize a million more people each year nationally by 2034.

APPENDIX B: *Endorsement*

Endorsement by former director of state evangelism:

The Church Missionary Movement represents a unique approach enabling a church to move forward in reaching the unchurched. This approach was first implemented and proven effective at College Heights Baptist Church in Gallatin, Tennessee in 1990 when Brent Lay served on our staff and I served as the Senior Pastor.

The church missionaries commit to training and accountability, intentionally focusing on outreach to a few families at a time, and receive a stipend for their investment of time in outreach ministry. A church will track and see measurable results from such an approach. The increased diversity of our culture calls us to a greater understanding of and focus on those we are seeking to reach.

I wholly endorse this evangelistic strategy and encourage you to invest in this approach.

Dr. Larry Gilmore, D. Min.

Former Director of Evangelism
(2003-2012)
Tennessee Baptist Convention

Five Key Questions and Answers:

1. **Are you suggesting that smaller churches generally grow differently than large churches?** If we define larger churches as those who average 400 or more in average attendance, the answer is yes. Larger churches can grow with the attraction model as they have capacity to have the very best worship services with staffing and technology and also more extensive age group ministries. The mistake of many smaller churches is trying to duplicate that same approach.

2. **With thousands of Southern Baptist Churches predicted to close over the next ten years, do you really think most of these churches can reverse course?** Yes, I believe the majority of these churches can become healthy again. Even with two church missionaries, reaching an additional 10 family units each year and baptizing 10 each year is very doable.

3. **Are you saying that most of these dying churches can return to being like they were?** The answer is no because our culture continues to change at a rapid pace. As our churches become more missional (defined as more focused upon intensive individualized outreach), I think our churches will be more flexible in their programming. The post-Covid-19 era will most

likely result in many continuing to watch worship services online. Effective methods of keeping church families connected will be even more important. The great news is most of our church buildings are already paid for allowing more investment in connection ministries. The smallest of churches with even 15 to 20 active members can support a bi-vocational pastor and two church missionaries and routinely reach 10 family units each year. This will result usually in about ten baptisms each year (based on 27 years of experience). Please remember that there is always six months to a year lag time to allow for the training and ramping up of this evangelism approach.

4. **Why has this strategy not been adopted by more churches already?** For one reason, it is completely different from approaches of the past. Secondly, many of our influential pastors are great preachers and it is only natural they feel great worship services are the key. No doubt, over the last forty years most of our churches have improved the overall quality of their worship services. This has worked well for some churches to attract church members from other churches, but we must remember that most of the unchurched do not necessarily have a worship style preference because they do not go to church nor feel the need to attend church. As result, the greater investment in quality worship services and age group programing has had a tendency for the larger churches to grow at the

expense of smaller churches. One of the main reasons the baptisms for Southern Baptists are at a 50-year low is because we have fewer lost people attending our worship services.

5. **Do you feel that the younger generation responds well to the church missionary approach?** The institutionalization of the church with huge investments in buildings has not fared well with the younger generation. All indications are that they are more attracted to being on mission. They value their time highly so staying connected in the most efficient manner is very attractive to their lifestyle. A key feature of the church missionary approach is the ability to adapt and adjust strategy on a week-to-week basis. What may have worked yesterday may be obsolete tomorrow. As the apostle Paul said, "I am made all things to all men that I might by all means save some." (1 Corinthians 9:22 b). The Apartment Life Ministry based in Euless, Texas is similar to this church missionary approach in that it involves 6 to 10 hours per week of the coordinator's time connecting people within apartment complexes. This ministry has grown exponentially since year 2000 and is currently in 30 states serving more than three million residents. This success with these who are mostly younger affirms that the young generation responds very well to connection opportunities.

APPENDIX D: *Any Hard Data Which Affirms?*

This ministry is really about the people the numbers represent. However, some insist that hard data should reflect the effectiveness of this ministry approach. The following data can be documented through the Tennessee Baptist Convention Annual Church Profile history. The following two examples are the best comparisons as the Pastors remained the same before and during the time this ministry approach was initiated.

A. **Englewood Baptist Church** in Jackson, Tennessee. Three years of 1994-1996 compared to three years of 1997-1999. This is significant because 1997-1999 represents the first three years of deploying this part-time outreach staffing at Englewood. During this three year period, as many as six people were part-time and meeting each week on Tuesdays at a 2 p.m. at the outreach meeting. The annual average in baptisms increased from 46 (94'-96') to 86 (97'-99') which was **an increase of 87%**. Even more confirmation was that the average small group attendance grew from 738 average attendance (94' to 97') to 933 average attendance (97' to 99') or 26%. This represents one of the most dramatic three year growth periods in the 70 year history of the church. The growth in small group attendance grew from 767 average in 1996 to 1,013 in 1999. This was **a 32% increase!** Special tribute to those who gave leadership to this effort during these years including Sarah

Coughlin, Doug Godfrey, Wanda Buford, Carol Courtner and Holly Adcock, who all served part-time multiple years. Wanda Buford served very effectively in this part-time ministry for 13 years.

B. **First Baptist Humboldt** (now is known as **The Church at Sugar Creek**) This outreach approach was initiated as part of The West Tennessee Innovative Evangelism project funded in part with $2,500 of the Golden Offering (state missions fund) as matching funds in 2009. Since, this was an Evangelism project designed to demonstrate this new strategy, the comparative number of baptisms for each year was a key measure.

Two years previous to the impact of this approach (2009-10), the average in baptisms per year was 15. During the two years of impact (after the training of two part-time people and ramping up this ministry in 2010) the average in baptisms per year grew to 26. This was **an increase of 73%.** During the two years following the project, the average in baptisms per year was 18. Note this is similar to a controlled study as circumstances stayed relatively the same with data collected before, during and after the use of this approach. Special tribute to Mike Sanders and Kathy Morris who served together during this demonstration project. In 2012, Mike became pastor at Hickory Grove Baptist Church in Trenton, Tennessee.

APPENDIX E. *Bringing this Ministry to Your Church*

How to begin this ministry for your church:

1. Review and study all the information on the website: churchmissionarymovement.com or connectionministy.org or growchurchgrow.org (all links lead to one web site).

2. Form a church missionary team (at least on an exploratory basis) of 3 to 9 members to explore the possibility of launching this ministry for your church. It is best that members of this team be evangelistic and missionary minded.

3. Order additional *"Revival and Survival of Stump Creek"* books from Amazon as needed for all team members. Books are priced at cost as this is a not-for-profit ministry (published as Kindle book also).

4. Continue to pray as you work through the entire book as a team. It is recommended that the church missionary team meet and discuss a few chapters at each setting. Question and Answer Study guides can be found on the web site in order that you may download and make copies for each team member.

5. You tube video training sessions should be available before January of 2022. If you have further questions, you may contact Brent Lay by sending an email to brentlay707@gmail.com. He or his representative will respond or refer as their ministry load will allow.

APPENDIX F: *Million More by '34 Handout*

MILLION MORE BY '34

GOING MISSIONAL WITH CHURCH MISSIONARY MOVEMENT

Going Missional
Adopting a concerted and continuous strategy
as a church to cross cultural barriers with the
Gospel of Jesus Christ.

- Involves highly trained part time Church Missionaries (8 to 10 hours per wk.)
- Easy for any size church to adopt this strategy without making major changes
- Involves concerted prayer for individuals
- Based on 27 years of proven success with 28 people serving in 6 different churches
- Highest and best use of volunteers
- Does not require additional time on behalf of Pastor
- Superior discipleship in that the one who reaches is also the primary one who teaches, disciples, and holds accountable.

Church Missionary
Highly trained person called by God, connected to
the local church, to cross cultural barriers for the
cause of the Gospel of Jesus Christ

127

APPENDIX G: *Ministry Description*

Church Missionary or Connection Coordinator Ministry Description

Part-time position for approximately 8 to 10 hours each week in addition to regular church schedule (expected to be present at least. 80% of the time for all major events).

Objective: That this person plays an instrumental role in having 5 or more family units join our church each year.

Duties include:
- **A.** Locating and discovering families who do not attend church on a regular basis.
- **B.** Maintaining contact with 8 to 10 families on a week-to-week basis.
- **C.** Acting as a host for special events for these families as well as inviting them to fellowship events at and away from the church building (usually once per month).
- **D.** Becoming a "next best friend" to families as you seek to connect them to other friends within the church family.
- **E.** Praying for each family member and witnessing to them as the relationship develops.
- **F.** Meeting on a weekly basis with at least a portion of the Church Missionary Team in order to gain insights on the most effective strategy to best connect each prospect with church member/s.

www.millionmoreby34.com
www.churchmissionarymovement.com

Made in the USA
Columbia, SC
02 November 2021

48223770R00074